Washtenaw Library for the Blind and Physically Disabled @ AADL

If you are only able to read large print, you may qualify for WLBPD @ AADL services, including receiving audio and large print books by mail at no charge.

For more information:

Email wlbpd@aadl.org
Phone (734) 327-4224
Website wlbpd.aadl.org

A Cowboy for Christmas

Also by Marcia Lynn McClure and available from Center Point Large Print:

Dusty Britches
Weathered Too Young
The Windswept Flame
The Visions of Ransom Lake
The Heavenly Surrender
The Light of the Lovers' Moon
Beneath the Honeysuckle Vine
The Whispered Kiss
The Stone-Cold Heart of Valentine Brisco
The Highwayman of Tanglewood

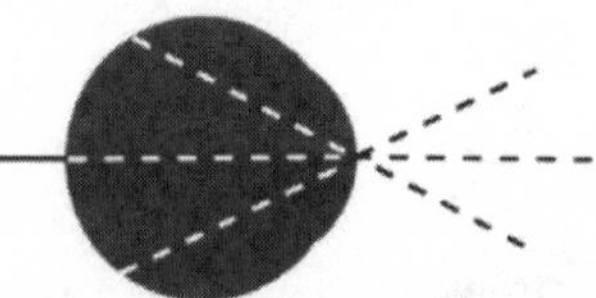

This Large Print Book carries the Seal of Approval of N.A.V.H.

A Cowboy for *Christmas*

Marcia Lynn McClure

Center Point Large Print
Thorndike, Maine

This Center Point Large Print edition
is published in the year 2018 by arrangement with
Distractions Ink.

The text of this Large Print edition is unabridged.
In other aspects, this book may vary
from the original edition.
Printed in the United States of America
on permanent paper.
Set in 16-point Times New Roman type.

ISBN: 978-1-68324-993-1

Library of Congress Cataloging-in-Publication Data

Names: McClure, Marcia Lynn, author.
Title: A cowboy for Christmas / Marcia Lynn McClure.
Description: Center Point Large Print edition. | Thorndike, Maine :
Center Point Large Print, 2018.
Identifiers: LCCN 2018036885 | ISBN 9781683249931
(hardcover : alk. paper)
Subjects: LCSH: Romance fiction. | Western stories. | Large type books.
Classification: LCC PS3613.C36 C69 2018 | DDC 813/.6—dc23
LC record available at https://lccn.loc.gov/2018036885

My everlasting admiration,
gratitude and love . . .
To my husband, Kevin . . .
My inspiration . . .
My heart's desire . . .
The man of my every dream!

To YOU!
Have a Very Merry Christmas!
~Marcia Lynn McClure

CHAPTER ONE

"Whoo-eee!" Bill Dickerson exclaimed as he burst through the front door. "I'll tell you one thing—it's colder than a witch's kiss out there tonight!"

Savannah watched as her stepfather removed his hat, scarf, and coat. Although his demeanor was jolly, his reminding his family of how cold it was outside caused an involuntary shiver to travel up Savannah's spine.

Bill stomped his snowy boots on the old rug Savannah's mother had placed to one side of the door. "Whoo!" Bill puffed again. "My nose hairs are frozen stiff!"

Savannah smiled, admittedly amused, as Bill pulled off his boots. Leaving them on the old rug, he rather trotted across the floor in his stocking feet to stand near the cookstove to warm himself.

"Did you get the ice in the trough all busted up for the cattle, Daddy?" Everett asked.

Bill hunkered down in front of Savannah's little brother, tousled his already tousled hair, and answered, "I sure did, son. It'll take it most of the night to freeze over again, so them cows will be fine. No worries, all righty?"

Everett smiled and nodded his assurance that he would try not to worry about the cattle.

"It sure does smell good in here, Lottie!" Bill exclaimed. He lifted the lid to the pot that was simmering on the stove. "Mmm-mmm! I love your beef stew, honey."

Savannah watched as her mother smiled with delight. Bill kissed his wife on the cheek and then turned to greet his daughters.

"And what are my girls up to this evenin'?" he asked.

Bill winked at Savannah as he turned his back to the stove once more to continue warming his backside.

"We're workin' on Christmas things, Daddy," Amelia said with a giggle.

Amelia was Bill Dickerson's youngest daughter. She was fourteen and more accepting of the new family dynamics than her older sister Sadie was.

"Still?" Bill playfully explained. "Why, I swear you girls have been workin' on Christmas for a month!"

"We have, Daddy," Sadie reminded him. "That's most of the fun—workin' on gifts and decorations for the tree and all. You know that."

Bill's eyebrows arched as he feigned astonishment. "I suppose so." He looked to Savannah then, asking, "And what're you workin' on there, Savannah sugar?"

"Me? Well, I'm just darnin' a few of Everett's socks," she answered. Smiling at her little brother, she added, "He wears holes in them faster than I can darn sometimes."

"All boys do," Bill said. Smiling at Everett, he chuckled, "Ain't that right, boy?" Everett nodded emphatically, wrapping his arms around Bill's waist as Bill added, "Let me warm up here a bit by the stove. Then you and me will sit down to a game of dominoes. Would ya like that?"

"Yes, indeed!" Everett exclaimed.

Savannah smiled when her mother smiled at her, as an unspoken understanding passed between them—knowing that Everett truly needed a father and that Bill was just that to him.

"Daddy," Sadie began as she sat working on a doily she was making.

"Yes, darlin'?" Bill responded in letting her know he was listening.

"Do you think this weather will clear a bit in time for the town social?" Sadie inquired. "I've just been lookin' so forward to it all year long! Whatever will I do if we can't get to town to attend?"

Sadie was nineteen—a year older than Savannah—and she never missed an opportunity to remind Savannah of the fact. Oh, Sadie wasn't cruel, per se—just a bit too bossy. She was pretty, that was for certain. Both Sadie and her younger sister, Amelia, owned hair the color of obsidian, beautiful sky-blue eyes, porcelain complexions, and slender figures. Savannah could see their resemblance to their father, Bill, and she surmised Bill's hair had once been the color of midnight too. His hair was what her mother referred to as a "distinguished salt with pepper" color now, and he had deep crow's-feet at the corners of his still sky-blue eyes. Savannah thought Bill to be a very handsome man and was happy her mother had found new happiness with him.

Yet as Savannah glanced to Everett, she smiled, her heart warmed by the fact that he was the spitting image of their father—and that she would always be able to remember exactly what her father looked like because of his reflection in her little brother's face.

Savannah choked back the tears that welled in her eyes at the thought of her father. Everett was so little when their father had been killed that he hardly remembered him at all. But Savannah had been fourteen—exactly the age Amelia was now—when her father had been killed while moving his cattle—and oh, how she missed him!

Jim Ambrose had been not only a great cattleman (though his ranch was small by most standards) but also a loving husband and father—a man of integrity and a refreshing sense of humor. Savannah's father had been tall and handsome with hair the color of warm straw and eyes as green as aspen leaves in summer.

Savannah envied Everett for having their father's straw-colored hair—especially since her mother had married Bill Dickerson. With Bill, Sadie, and Amelia boasting hair the color of night, Everett looking like a startled scarecrow half the time with his ever-tousled blond hair. And with Savannah's own mother owning hair as soft and as dark as sable, Savannah certainly felt dowdy and plain with her own rather hazelnut brown head of hair. Oh, Savannah liked her hair well enough, but it wasn't at all striking or unique—just brown. At least she had her father's eyes, although Everett's were a brighter green than her own. Still, she could see her father in them, and that was something to cling to in times of missing him so desperately.

Bill was a kind, affectionate, happy, and loving man, and Savannah loved him in a way. But he could never fill the empty hole in her heart her father had left when he'd died.

"Oh, I'm sure the weather will be fine, Sadie Sue," Bill reassured his eldest daughter.

Bill's response drew Savannah from her darker thoughts, for she knew Sadie would not be satisfied with such a flimsy response.

"You're just puttin' me off, Daddy," Sadie grumbled, scowling. "You know how important the Christmas social is to me! I swear I'll just *die* if somethin' happens to keep us from goin' this year!"

"Oh, you ain't gonna die if we don't make the social," Bill said, trying not to smile and thereby giving away that he thought Sadie's dramatics were amusing. "Why, you don't hear Savannah here goin' on and on about dyin' if we can't make it—Amelia or Everett neither—and I'm sure they wanna go just as bad as you do, darlin'." Bill winked at Savannah, and she smiled, comforted by his affection for her. He was, after all, the best stepfather any young woman and her little brother could've hoped for. He treated Savannah and Everett exactly as if they were his own and he'd helped raise them since birth. Savannah not only loved him for his kindness and acceptance of her and Everett, but she respected him for it too.

"Well, that's because Amelia and Savannah aren't in love," Sadie whined. "Everett either."

"Hey there!" Everett exclaimed, however. "I am so in love! I wanna go to the social just as much as you!'

"And who are you in love with, sweet pea?" their mother, Lottie, asked. She reached down, rubbing a smudge of jam from the corner of his mouth with her thumb.

"I'm in love with cookies! And there's always plenty of cookies at Christmas socials. Ain't there, Daddy?" Everett explained with excitement.

Everyone laughed quietly, and Bill chuckled, "Damn right there are, son! Plenty of cookies . . . and all different kinds too."

Everett smiled—even snickered a little at Bill's swearing.

"Daddy, don't swear," Sadie scolded. "And lovin' cookies is very different than bein' *in* love, Everett."

Everett clasped his hands over his heart, batted his thick, straw-colored eyelashes, and in a higher-pitched voice said, "And lovin' cookies is very different than bein' in love, Everett," he quoted, mimicking Sadie. "And I'm in love with Clay Picket! That's for sure and for certain!" he added.

"Everett," Lottie gently reprimanded, "don't you mock Sadie's feelin's. She cares very deeply for Clay Picket."

"And I care very deeply for cookies," Everett added. "I want to go to the Christmas social too, Sadie. So don't think you're the only one who's worried about a storm comin' in and keepin' us away."

"We all want to go to the social," Bill said. His voice was firm—a signal that he wanted the nonsense to subside. "So we'll hope and pray for the best and see what happens when the time comes." He smiled, turned, and took Lottie by the waist. "I mean, I want to go to the social too . . . so's I can catch your pretty mama under the mistletoe and do a little sparkin', right there in public."

Savannah smiled as her mother blushed with delight. It was so wonderful to see her mother happy once more. It was wonderful to know there was a man who cared enough for them all to make sure they were warm, fed, and comfortable—cared for—and not just through winter but always.

The kitchen was warm, fragrant with the comforting aromas of simmering stew and bread fresh from the oven. From where she sat at the kitchen table, working so diligently in an attempt to stretch Everett's pathetically holey socks to a few more weeks of wear, Savannah could see the beautiful pine tree Bill and Everett had chopped down and hauled into the house several days before. It looked so beautiful sitting in the front parlor window. Naturally the candles on the tree were not lit, being that they must be saved for Christmas Eve to enjoy. Still, the tree stood bedecked with strings of popcorn, happy gingerbread men, red holly berries, all the different bits of ribbon Savannah, Sadie, and Amelia could gather, and even several tiny cornhusk dolls Savannah's mother had fashioned. Bill had carved a beautiful star to set atop the tree, and Savannah thought that it was indeed the tree's crowning glory. She thought of the new star that appeared in the heavens to announce the Lord's birth, and it made her smile.

"Oh, I do hope everyone enjoys the gifts I've made," Amelia sighed. "I just don't have the skill with sewin' and knittin' that Sadie does, or Savannah, and I'm so afraid my gifts will pale in comparison."

Savannah smiled at her young stepsister. "Your sewin and knittin' are wonderful, Amelia. And whatever you've made for me, I will love it—because you made it just for me! It could be the homeliest ragdoll the world has ever seen, and I would love it with all my heart and soul. So no more worries, hmmm? Gifts are best when they're from the heart . . . and homemade. Those are my favorite gifts of all."

"Well, what other kinds of gifts are there?" Everett asked. "I mean, Mama always makes me some new mittens or a hat or scarf. I always feel warmer in them because I know Mama made them for me. I draw'd some scenery for you last Christmas, Savannah. So what else is there?"

"I received a pair of new shoes from Daddy for my birthday this past summer," Amelia remarked, "and a bracelet made of real silver from my grandpa last Christmas. Things like that—store-bought things—they're so pretty and nice."

"Well, certainly they are," Sadie began, "but I agree with Savannah. Something stitched or knitted or carved . . ." She leaned over from her chair, kissing Everett square on one cheek. "Or a pretty drawin' of scenery—those are the best gifts of all. Even a kiss is a wonderful gift! Isn't that right, Everett?"

"I s'pose so," Everett grumbled, blushing and pretending to wipe Sadie's kiss from his cheek.

"Any gift is a wonderful thing," Lottie explained. "Handmade, store-bought, or givin' someone some help with something. All gifts are to be heartfelt and thought out when given, and appreciated and loved when accepted."

"That's right," Bill agreed emphatically. "And I'll tell you one thing. I happen to know that Santa Claus has got somethin' special he plans on bringin' to you, Everett."

Savannah giggled as Everett's eyes widened with excitement. "Really? How do you know? Did you write him a letter, Daddy? Did he write ya back?"

"I sure did . . . and he sure did," Bill affirmed. "I wrote ol' Santa a letter a long while back, askin' what he had in mind to bring my boy this year. And dang if he didn't send me a letter right back, tellin' me just what he had planned."

Everett gasped with delight. "Did you hear that, Mama? Santa's comin' this year! He didn't forget me just 'cause we moved up here when you married Daddy! Did you hear that, Mama? Daddy's been writin' to Santa and everything!"

Lottie laughed, and Savannah could see the joy

in her mother's eyes. "Yes, honey, I heard," she assured her son.

"What about for the girls, Daddy?" Everett asked then. "Did you write to Santa about all my sisters?"

Bill nodded, answering, "I surely did! And Santa said he's got plans for the girls too."

"All I want for Christmas is Clay Picket," Sadie said, smiling. "And if Santa can work that out . . . well, I really will be surprised on Christmas mornin'!"

Everyone but Everett laughed. But Everett frowned and said, "Sadie, I don't think Clay Picket will fit in Santa's sack . . . or down our chimney either."

"Oh, Santa has his ways," Sadie assured Everett, however. "If he wanted to bring Clay Picket to me for Christmas, then I know he'd find a way."

"Is that true?" Everett asked Bill.

Bill tousled Everett's straw hair again. "Yep—though I think Santa is more'n likely to bring Sadie some peppermint hard candies for her stockin'." Bill chuckled. "But can't you just imagine, Everett? Us all gettin' up Christmas mornin' to find Clay Picket tied up and waitin' under the Christmas tree?"

Everett burst into giggling. "Oh, what a sight that would be!"

Even Sadie laughed, sighing, "Oh, Daddy! You are so funny sometimes!"

A very loud pounding on the door startled everyone then.

"Well, who on earth could that be at this hour? And in this weather?" Lottie asked. "I swear, that knockin' nearly startled me right out of my skin!"

"Me too, Mama," Savannah agreed. In fact, her heart was still racing.

"We aren't expectin' anyone, are we, Lottie?" Bill asked.

"No. Not at all," Lottie said.

Savannah watched as Bill quickly strode toward the door. He grabbed the rifle he'd set next to it when he'd entered earlier and then called, "Hello? Who's that?"

A deep, masculine voice answered from the other side of the door. "Mr. Dickerson? It's me, Trenner Barnett. Do you remember me, sir?"

"Trenner Barnett?" Bill mumbled, frowning as he immediately pulled the bolt on the door and opened it.

A gust of merciless wind and blowing snow whooshed into the house in the wake of the man who stepped in.

"For cryin' out loud, Trenner!" Bill exclaimed, closing the door behind the man. "How the hell are you, boy? And what on earth are you doin' out this way? And in weather the likes of this?"

Savannah felt her eyes widen as she looked at the man who'd literally been blown into the house. He was very tall, dressed for winter in a heavy coat, jeans, and boots. When he took off his hat, however, Savannah felt her heart leap in her chest—for the man was extraordinarily handsome! He had brown hair, flattened against his head from perspiration and wearing his hat. His eyes were dark—so dark they looked almost black in that she could not discern his pupils from the rest of his dark eyes. His nose was straight and not big nor small, and his chin and jaw were square, with perfectly masculine angles.

"I'm winterin' out at the Colbalt place just south of Adamsville," the man began to explain. "And this mornin' I come upon some rustlers cuttin' out a good bit of cattle, probably fifteen head at least. I knew the weather was comin' in hard, and so did all the other boys . . . which is why no one went with me to try and follow them sons of—" Trenner Barnett glanced to Savannah's mother and then continued, ". . . them rustlers. So I followed them on my own, hopin' they'd bunk down for the night or somethin' and I could just . . . I guess just beat them bloody and take the cattle back. You know I ride for the brand, Mr. Dickerson, and I needed to get them cattle back to Mr. Colbalt." The cowboy inhaled a deep breath.

"I take it there's a but in there somewhere?" Bill urged.

Trenner Barnett nodded. "Yes, sir, there is," he said. "They must've caught wind of me or somethin' about five miles back, 'cause all at once they started shootin' at me. I think I got hit a couple of times. I haven't really looked yet. But with this storm comin' in like a monster, I've gotta give it up for the night. So I was wonderin' if you maybe have an extra bed in your bunkhouse where I could sit it out. I'll probably lose their trail because of the wind and snow, but I'd still like to head out after them in the mornin'. I can pay for my bunk, and it would just be for the night."

Bill was silent for a moment—nodded as if considering whether to let the man stay in the bunkhouse. When he spoke, he said, "Boy, I'll tell you one thing, and that is that you are loco! You can't be goin' after rustlers on your own! You oughta know better'n that. But you always were the hardest-workin', most honest man I ever come across. So I gotta say I ain't surprised. And of course you can bunk here for the night, although I figure we oughta look you over a bit first. You're sweatin' like a horse, even for ridin' hard."

"Thank you, sir," Trenner said. Savannah discerned that, even though the man was trying to appear strong and calm, he was very grateful for Bill's generosity—and that he was most likely feverish. "But I'll just head on out to the bunkhouse and patch myself up there, sir. I'm already puttin' you out enough over this."

"Nonsense!" Lottie exclaimed, striding across the room to the man. "You don't look well at all, Mr. Barnett. Let's have a better look at you."

"Well, his leg is bleedin', for one thing," Everett said, pointing to the man's right leg.

"Yep. And he's bleedin' over here on this left arm as well," Bill sighed. He chuckled, shaking his head in astonishment. "Boy, you are somethin' else. I always said I'd rather have one Trenner Barnett working my ranch than five other cowboys. You're tough as nails, son."

"I'm sure I've only been grazed, ma'am," Trenner said to Lottie. "It's nothin' a little soap and a needle and thread can't patch up."

"I won't hear of it," Lottie said, however. "Now remove your coat and boots, and we'll see how bad things are on you. Then you can sit down and have some supper with us before you rest. All right?"

Trenner Barnett grinned, and Savannah felt her own lips curl into a smile of delight at the sight of how even more handsome he became when he was pleased.

"I'm thinkin' you married this wonderful woman, Mr. Dickerson," he said.

He glanced to Everett and then Savannah. Savannah could've sworn Trenner's gaze lingered on her a little longer than was necessary, and it unsettled her greatly. Pleased her—but unsettled her.

"Added a couple more kittens to the litter too, hmm?" Trenner asked.

"I sure did!" Bill exclaimed. "This here is Lottie, my beautiful wife," he said, motioning to Lottie.

Trenner removed his right glove and shook Lottie's hand. "Pleased to meet you, ma'am," he said.

"And this here's my son, Everett, and my daughter Savannah," Bill continued.

"Everett," Trenner said, shaking Everett's hand when the boy offered it to him. He then nodded toward Savannah and said, "Miss."

"And of course you remember Sadie and Amelia," Bill added.

"I sure do," Trenner said. He smiled at Sadie and then Amelia, greeting, "Evenin', ladies. You two sure have grown up since last time I was here."

Savannah watched as both Sadie and Amelia blushed. It was clear that they both remembered Trenner Barnett—that they both found him attractive, as well. No doubt both Dickerson girls had found themselves mooning over the handsome cowboy like lovesick puppies in years past.

"Now take that coat off, young man," Lottie gently demanded, "and let's see how grisly your wounds really are."

Trenner placed his hat on the hat rack near the

front door. He removed his other glove, stuffing both gloves in one coat pocket before removing his coat and hanging it on a hook on the wall.

"Boots too," Lottie instructed, "although you'll probably need to strip off your trousers for me to have a look at that leg."

"Let's just start with my arm, if you don't mind," Trenner said, glancing to where Sadie, Amelia, and Savannah sat at the kitchen table.

Lottie smiled. "All right. We'll tend to your arm first."

Savannah watched—found herself holding her breath with trepidation as her mother looked at the cowboy's left arm.

"Well, it's more than a graze, Mr. Barnett," Lottie said, frowning. "You'll need to remove your shirt so I can get a better look at it."

"Yes, ma'am," Trenner mumbled.

Savannah's eyes widened as the cowboy began to unbutton the front of his shirt—widened further when he stripped it off to reveal he was wearing nothing underneath it.

She glanced to see Sadie's and Amelia's eyes were as wide as her own, both of their mouths gaping open slightly in amazement.

"You sure got a lot of muscles, mister!" Everett noted.

Bill looked to Savannah and his own daughters and chuckled, "You sure do, Trenner."

"Savannah," Lottie began, "please run get some

rags for bandages out of my ragbag. And, Sadie, will you put some water on to boil? And I'll need my sewin' things, if you wouldn't mind fetchin' those for me, Amelia."

All three girls nodded their affirmations that they would do as Lottie asked. Yet all three still sat staring in awed wonder at the half-naked cowboy standing in the kitchen.

"Sooner than later, ladies," Lottie urged when she realized the girls hadn't moved a twitch.

"Yes, Mama," Savannah said, hopping up from her chair and hurrying toward the back room where her mother kept the ragbag.

"I got somethin' I gotta do real quick too, Mama," Everett said.

"All right, honey. But come right back. We might need your help," Lottie said, winking at her young son.

"You bet, Mama! I wouldn't miss this bloody mess for anything!" Everett exclaimed as he hightailed it down the hall toward his bedroom.

Everett ducked into his room, closing the door behind him. And although Savannah had a fleeting thought of wondering what in the world her little brother could need out of his room at a time like this, she was too distracted with thoughts and concerns for Mr. Barnett's well-being. She'd seen her mother's face when she'd inspected the wound on the man's arm—an expression of deep worry. Therefore, Savannah knew the cowboy's injuries weren't as mild as he was trying to let on.

"Dang, that man is good-lookin'!" she exclaimed to herself as she began rummaging through the flour sack full of rags her mother kept in the back room. Savannah shook her head, trying to dispel the images of Trenner Barnett standing in the kitchen all windblown and shirtless—but she couldn't. Everett had been right: Mr. Barnett was very, very muscular, very broad-shouldered, and very without the proper underclothing for winter! The thought flittered through Savannah's mind that if Trenner Barnett wasn't wearing long johns—which was obvious by his bareness from the waist up—then what was he wearing under his trousers? It was a shocking thought and very inappropriate. Therefore, Savannah simply began to hum "Shall We Gather at the River?" as she searched for just the right rags to serve as bandages for the handsome cowboy in the kitchen.

Dropping to his knees at his bedside, Everett bowed his head, clasped his hands together, and rested his elbows on his bed. Closing his eyes, he whispered, "Thank you, Lord! Thank you, thank you, thank you! When I prayed the other night for you to send a cowboy for Savannah . . . well, I guess I didn't know how quick you work your miracles, sometimes! Thank you for sendin' this cowboy for my sister. I know I told you already how much she needs her own man to love and to love her back, especially since Mama married Bill. And Trenner Barnett is perfect, Lord! So thank you so much! And thank God for me too, while you're at it! Also, I don't need nothin' else for Christmas, at all! Sendin' Trenner Barnett for Savannah is all I ever need. Of course, if you have some extra time to speak to Santa Claus, I could use a new saddle all my own. But that's only if you have time and think it's important enough. I know you got a lot more things and a lot more people to worry about, 'specially this time of year. So I'll thank you again, Lord . . . for the cowboy for Christmas. Yours truly, Everett Ambrose. Amen!"

Hopping up from his knees, Everett raced like a jackrabbit out of his room and back to the kitchen. His prayers for Savannah had been answered! And now—well, he didn't want to miss a moment more of seeing what kind of bloody wounds the cowboy in the kitchen might have for him to look at.

CHAPTER TWO

"You're fortunate both bullets went through and through, Mr. Barnett," Lottie said as she finished dressing the wound on Trenner's leg. "But your fever concerns me greatly."

Savannah's frown had been perpetual since the moment her mother had begun working on the wounded cowboy. Even though the two bullets had not come to rest in his arm or leg or struck bone, Savannah knew the danger of infection was high. Furthermore, the fact that Mr. Barnett was already feverish was very worrisome. Her mother had listened to his breathing and was fairly certain pneumonia had not set in—not yet, at least. But Savannah knew that more cowboys died of pneumonia than from any other cause. Therefore, a great trepidation had settled inside Savannah over the state of Mr. Barnett's health.

Trenner Barnett now sat in a kitchen chair wearing only his socks and long underwear. The truth was, Savannah had felt a mild, sinfully prideful sense of triumph when her mother had asked Sadie and Amelia to leave the room while Mr. Barnett removed his jeans, yet had asked

Savannah to stay to assist her. It was not an act of favoritism in the least—just practicality, being that Savannah had assisted her mother tending to many wounds on many various people during her life. Still, once Trenner had stepped out of his jeans to reveal that he was indeed wearing a pair of long underwear pants beneath them, Savannah surmised her mother was worried about offending her two stepdaughters when she asked Sadie and Amelia to return to assist, as well.

As for Trenner Barnett, he seemed quite uncomfortable sitting in nothing but his underwear in a room full of women. Bill eased the cowboy's mind by teasing him that any man would relish such an experience—being tended to and mollycoddled by four beautiful women. For Everett's part, he just couldn't get enough of gawking at Trenner's wounds and pummeling him with questions the likes of, "Can you feel the blood runnin' down your leg, mister? 'Cause it's runnin' down right now!"

Still, the cowboy took everything in stride, or seemed to—although Savannah wasn't sure if it was because he was simply easy-going or because his fever was getting worse and worse. But the one thing she did know was that he was truly something to behold!

Savannah had grown up around cowboys, for cowboys had always worked for her father on the ranch. But no other cowboy she'd ever met was as handsome, as tall, as strong, and as capable-looking as Trenner Barnett was. It was obvious that Sadie and Amelia were just as affected by the man's presence as Savannah was, and she secretly envied them both for knowing him so well already.

Once or twice, Trenner glanced to Savannah as she helped her mother with his wounds. Both times, the dark warmth of his gaze caused butterflies to swarm in Savannah's stomach. She was embarrassed by her body's reaction to the man—goose bumps when she touched him, butterflies in her stomach when he looked at her. It was ridiculous to her that she should be so disconcerted by a stranger. Yet she couldn't seem to help herself—couldn't keep her arms from racing with goose bumps, couldn't make the butterflies settle in her stomach.

And so Savannah simply feigned calmness as she helped tend to the wounded, sick cowboy.

"How long have you been feverish, Mr. Barnett?" Lottie asked as she finished binding the wound on Trenner's leg.

"Wasn't aware that I was, ma'am. Sorry," Trenner answered.

Lottie smiled, patting Trenner's cheek as if he were no older than Everett. "That's nothin' to be sorry for, honey. But we best get some stew down your gullet and get you tucked into a warm bed so you can rest. We need to watch these wounds for infection and that fever for . . ." Pausing, Lottie looked to Sadie, asking, "Would you ladle up some stew for Mr. Barnett please, Sadie? The man's got to be starvin'."

"Of course," Sadie agreed, smiling at Trenner.

Savannah held her breath for a moment, thought maybe she was losing her wits, for as Sadie handed Trenner Barnett a bowl of steaming stew—as he looked at her, saying, "Thank you, Miss Sadie," and as Sadie said, "You're very welcome, Trenner"—such a wave of jealousy crashed over Savannah, she nearly screamed.

Savannah didn't know the man from a badger's back end! Yet somehow she was developing an insatiable sort of infatuation with him. He'd been in the house no more than an hour, but Savannah had feelings of never wanting him to leave.

Thankful when her mother gave her the task of preparing Everett's room for Trenner Barnett to stay the night in (no matter how firmly yet politely the cowboy kept insisting he could not and would not stay in the house), Savannah tried to steady her uneven breathing as she stripped the sheets from Everett's bed. What on earth was wrong with her? she kept wondering, however. The man was a stranger to her! Why would she be so instantly attracted to him? Well, she could understand the instant attraction, for the man was unbelievably handsome. But Savannah wasn't the type of girl to place her hopes and heart on something simply because it was alluring or beautiful. So what was wrong with her?

As she spread clean sheets on Everett's bed, Savannah wondered whether perhaps she were just lonesome. Life had changed when her mother had married Bill—drastically changed. Certainly many of the changes were welcome and joyous and provided reassurance to Savannah. After all, her mother was happy and loved once more and didn't have the constant worry about how to provide food and shelter for Savannah and Everett. Everett and Savannah were loved and safe, as well. And Sadie and Amelia were kind and loving to her and Everett and seemed to have accepted them as new siblings almost instantly.

But in being honest with herself—in unleashing her deepest musings—Savannah *did* feel lonesome. It sounded ridiculous, she knew—to feel alone in a warm, happy houseful of people. But she did. And she wasn't so much lonesome for mere company as she was lonesome for—well, companionship or something. Perhaps it was simply the fact that she did see what her mother had now—someone to be in love with and to be in love with her in return, someone to laugh with, flirt with, someone to care for her as deeply as Bill did. Even Everett had a new sort of relationship—the father–son relationship he had been too young to remember, being that their father had been killed when Everett was so little.

But Savannah—Savannah just felt empty. Undoubtedly she didn't worry so much over the temporal well-being of her mother, brother, and herself as she had before her mother had met and married Bill. But the emptiness she felt now was much deeper than simply the need for food, clothing, and shelter. It was an aching, lonely emptiness.

As she spread the blankets and quilts over the surface of the freshly made bed, Savannah exhaled a heavy sigh. Could it be that she was so lonesome, so empty, so pathetic that some stranger showing up on the threshold a week before Christmas could steal her heart? Was she that ridiculous? That wretched?

Shaking her head and exhaling another sigh, Savannah breathed, "You're just tired," out loud to herself. "You can never think straight when you're overly tired, Savannah Ambrose."

Feeling somewhat better, having found a reason for her ludicrous musings where the cowboy in the kitchen was concerned, Savannah put her hands on her hips, admiring how nice and comfortable Everett's bed appeared since she'd spruced it up.

As she turned to leave the room, however, she gasped, finding herself breathless—for there in the doorway, one of his muscular arms propped around Bill's shoulders, stood Trenner Barnett in all his masculine perfection.

"Ma'am, I ain't fit to sleep in the house here—" Trenner said.

"Nonsense," Lottie scolded as she followed Bill and Trenner into the room. "I won't have you out in that drafty old bunkhouse when you're with fever."

"Should I get a fire goin' in here, Mama?" Everett asked as he skittered into the room.

"Yes, please, Everett," Lottie said. "But a small one. We don't want Mr. Barnett overheated either."

"Savannah," Bill said, "here, hold him up a minute while I help your mama."

"What?" Savannah asked, her eyes widening as Trenner's two large hands came to rest on her shoulders when Bill released him to help her mother turn down the bed.

"Hello there," the cowboy said as he looked down into Savannah's face. A grin quirked one corner of his mouth, and Savannah felt the unfamiliar warmth of desire fill hers.

"Hello," she managed to respond.

"Here you go, boy," Bill said then. "You get into this bed and sleep as long as you can. I know you, Trenner, and you'll want to be up and about before the sun. But you do what Mrs. Dickerson tells you, you hear me?"

"Yes, sir," Trenner said. "But I don't want Mr. Colbalt thinkin' I've run off—or worse, that I helped cut out that cattle that was rustled."

"I'll get to town in the mornin' and get a telegram off to him," Bill said. "Quit worryin' about such things. You need to rest."

Trenner still stood with his hands resting on Savannah's shoulders—still stood gazing down at her with half a grin—a grin of pleasure.

Savannah could feel his fever radiating from his palms, even through her blouse, and she felt bad for enjoying his touch when he was obviously ill.

"Now get on into bed, Mr. Barnett," Lottie instructed. "I'll have Everett bring you a bucket for under the bed. I don't want you tryin' to go traipsin' through this cold out to the privy."

"Oh, ma'am, I couldn't possibly," the cowboy began to argue.

"Into bed," Lottie demanded.

With one last rather lingering look at Savannah, Trenner turned, groaning as he climbed onto the bed.

"Mr. Dickerson," Trenner began, "I truly did not come here lookin' to impose like this."

"I know that, Trenner," Bill reassured the man. "But me and Lottie wouldn't sleep a wink with you out in the bunkhouse with that fever and bein' shot up the way you are. You know that."

"Yes, sir," Trenner said. "But I am truly sorry . . . especially to you and your girls, Mrs. Dickerson."

"It's nothing to apologize for, Mr. Barnett," Lottie reassured the man.

The small fire Everett had built in the hearth was already beginning to crackle, and Savannah knew the room would soon be toasty warm. With warm stew in his stomach, a fever, and the no doubt miserable ache of two bullet wounds, Savannah was sure Trenner Barnett would soon be sound asleep.

"Run get a bucket to put under the bed for Mr. Barnett please, Everett," Lottie instructed.

But Everett shrugged. "I don't need to. I already put one under there days ago when it started gettin' so cold out. I sure as heck wasn't goin' out to the privy in the middle of the night in this weather." Lowering his voice and speaking to Trenner, Everett added, "But don't worry. It's nice and clean 'cause I ain't had need of it yet."

Trenner chuckled, and the sound caused a thrill of delight to travel over Savannah's body.

"Thank you, Everett," Trenner said, smiling—smiling a mesmerizing, gorgeous smile. "I hope I don't have need of it neither, but it's good to know it's there, all the same."

"Now let's leave Mr. Barnett to his rest," Lottie suggested.

"I'll run get a glass of water for him, just in case he gets thirsty in the night, Mama," Everett said as he dashed from the room.

"All right. But then you leave the man be, do you hear me, Everett?" Lottie called after her son.

"Yes, Mama," Everett hollered from the hallway.

"Good night then, Trenner," Bill said. "Get some sleep, and I'll send that telegram to Colbalt first thing . . . weather permittin', that is."

"Yes, sir," Trenner said. "And thank you, Mrs. Dickerson. For everything. And the stew was delicious."

"You're welcome," Lottie said. "Now sleep tight, and holler if you need anything."

"Yes, ma'am," Trenner agreed—but Savannah could tell by the look on his face, and what she could already determine about his good character, that Trenner wouldn't holler for anyone to bring him anything or help him, even if red ants were eating him alive.

"Thank you too, Miss Savannah," Trenner said as Savannah turned to follow her mother and Bill out of the room. "This bed is the most comfortable I've known in a long while."

Savannah knew she was blushing as she turned to him and said, "I hope so. You need your rest."

"Yes, ma'am," he said, with a nod and a grin.

"Sleep well," Savannah added as the butterflies went loco in her stomach.

"You too, ma'am," Trenner said.

Savannah exhaled a sigh of elation as she left the room. He was truly marvelous!

As Everett came toward her carrying a glass of water and trying not to slosh it out all over the floor, he smiled at Savannah and whispered, "You think he's handsome, don't you, Savannah?"

Perplexed at her little brother's question, and at the same time worried that her admiration of Trenner Barnett was far too apparent if her little brother could see it, she nodded and answered, "He is handsome." Bending down to kiss her little brother on the cheek then, she added, "And so are you."

Everett shook his head. "You girls are so soppy sometimes."

Savannah giggled as she watched Everett hurry into his bedroom with the glass of water for the cowboy. Everett was so thoughtful, she mused. It was a quality she hoped he never lost.

"Here you go, mister," Everett said as he set the glass of water on the little table next to his bed. "Just in case you get thirsty in the night, you won't have to get up and go wanderin' around lookin' for a drink of water."

"Thank you kindly, Everett," the cowboy said, smiling at him.

"You remember my name!" Everett exclaimed with glee.

"Of course I do," the cowboy said. "I can tell you're a mighty big help to Mr. Dickerson . . . and your mother too. That makes a body remember you and your name with respect."

"It does?" Everett asked proudly.

"Yes, it does," the cowboy assured him.

"Well, you let me know if you need anything, mister," Everett began, "because now that you're here, I gotta make sure you stay well enough."

"Well enough for what?" the cowboy chuckled.

Everett rolled his eyes with exasperation. "You know, well enough to marry Savannah."

"What's that?" Trenner asked the boy. Had he heard the kid correctly—that Trenner had to stay well enough to *marry* the boy's sister?

Again Everett rolled his eyes. "I prayed for you! What? Are you ignorant or somethin'? I prayed to the Lord and Jesus that they would send a cowboy for Savannah to love . . . and then tonight, they sent you! You just blew in through the door, and here you are. Course, I didn't expect you to be all banged up like you are, but I suppose that's part of it."

"Boy, I can assure you that I ain't no answer to a prayer," Trenner said as kindly as he could. "I'm just a cowboy and—"

"I know! That's what I prayed for," Everett interrupted. The boy frowned a moment and then asked, "You do think Savannah's pretty, don't you?"

Trenner smiled at the thought of Mr. Dickerson's pretty stepdaughter. The girl was so much more attractive than Sadie and Amelia. For one thing, she was soft in her appearance—

approachable—with beautiful green eyes and a face like an angel.

"Of course she's pretty," Trenner admitted. "But that don't mean—"

Everett smiled and interjected, "And she thinks you're handsome too. So it's all perfect! You *are* the answer to my prayer for Savannah. And now I can quit worryin' about how Santy Claus was gonna haul you in through our chimney on Christmas Eve. What a relief that is to my mind. Now you sleep well and get better, mister. Christmas is only two weeks away. Good night!"

And as fast as that, the boy was gone, closing the door behind him and off to who knew what kind of mischief.

"Poor kid," Trenner mumbled to himself. For if there was one thing he was sure of, it was that he would never, could never, be an answer to a prayer.

"I had forgotten how handsome Trenner is!" Amelia said as she and Sadie and Savannah lay in their beds in their bedroom later that night.

"I hadn't," Sadie admitted. "When he walked through that door tonight . . . well, I swear I nearly forgot all about Clay Picket for a moment. But just for a moment, mind you."

Amelia and Sadie giggled, and Savannah even did too. The truth was that she liked having sisters and sharing a room with them.

Sadie and Amelia had both had their own bedrooms before Savannah's mother had married Bill, adding Savannah and Everett to the family. It had been an obvious change to make—all three girls sharing a room so that Everett, the only boy, would have his own—and Savannah was grateful that neither of her stepsisters seemed to mind not having their own sleeping space now.

Furthermore, all three girls had discussed the fact that sharing a room at night—conversing in lowered, almost secretive voices before going to sleep—was not only fun but also had drawn them all together more quickly than they might have otherwise found had they all been separated.

"What do you think, Savannah?" Amelia asked then. "Don't you think Trenner is handsome?"

"Oh, most definitely!" Savannah answered in a near whisper. "I can just see the two of you runnin' around after him like lovesick kittens when he worked for your daddy."

Amelia and Sadie both laughed quietly.

"Oh, you have no idea!" Sadie admitted. "It's quite the most embarrassin' thing to look back on . . . at least for me."

"Sadie used to want to marry Trenner," Amelia blurted.

"Hush, Amelia! That was a long time ago!" Sadie scolded.

"But you did! You wanted to marry Trenner Barnett so badly. I remember!" Amelia teased.

"Well, I have Clay now, and Clay is who I want to marry," Sadie said firmly. "And you're still too young for him, Amelia. So I guess . . ."

"Savannah will get to marry him!" Amelia giggled.

"Yes! Savannah, you need to marry Trenner Barnett! I mean, one of us girls has to have him, don't you think?" Sadie teased.

"I suppose you're right," Savannah said, joining in the silliness. "So . . . if I must, I must, right?"

"Oh, you must!" Amelia exclaimed, bursting into laughter.

Sadie began laughing as well, and Savannah found that she could no longer contain her own laughter. It felt so good to laugh! It was something that had been almost completely absent in her life for the years following her father's death. Thus, lying in bed in a warm, cozy bedroom, sharing silly talk, secrets, and laughter with Sadie and Amelia caused a great sense of peace and happiness to settle over her. And there was something else adding to her feelings of joy and tranquility—the fact that Trenner Barnett was in the room across the hallway. As utterly preposterous as it would have seemed to Sadie and Amelia if Savannah had had the courage to tell them about it, it was true! He was a stranger—though a handsome, strong, obviously capable stranger. Still, the cowboy across the hall *was* indeed a stranger to Savannah. Yet it comforted her to know he was in the house. And although Savannah didn't know what to make of such feelings—was far too confused herself about them to confide in Sadie and Amelia about them—the fact remained that she felt what she felt where Trenner Barnett was concerned.

And so, as Savannah, Sadie, and Amelia continued to chitchat and giggle for near to an hour before finally finding themselves sleepy enough to settle down, Savannah secretly bathed in the feelings of warm joy and cozy companionship—*and* in the secret delight she was feeling about the stranger convalescing across the hall.

CHAPTER THREE

"Everett," Lottie began as she placed the plate heaping with biscuits, eggs, and bacon on the serving tray, "will you please take this in to Mr. Barnett for me? I'm sure he's near starvin' to death by now."

"I sure will, Mama," Everett said, leaping up from his own seat at the table. He paused a moment, however, glancing to Savannah as an idea began to form in his mischievous little mind.

"Um . . . maybe Savannah oughta take it in, Mama," Everett suggested. "Or she should at least go with me, to make sure I don't spill nothin' or dump the tray out on Mr. Barnett's lap altogether."

Lottie's eyebrows arched as her imagination played out the possible scenarios Everett's suggestion had, no doubt, sent racing through her mind. Nodding, she said, "Savannah, would you please go with Everett to deliver Mr. Barnett's breakfast?"

Savannah giggled, for she could just imagine the mess that would ensue if Everett were to hurry too fast and drop the tray as he'd suggested. "Of course, Mama," Savannah agreed. Rising from her chair, she picked up the silver serving tray her mother had prepared. "Come along, Everett. I know you're fit to be tied with wantin' to see how Mr. Barnett fared the night."

"Oh, I am!" Everett admitted. "So come on, Savannah. And I do feel better with you carryin' the tray. But you best let me enter the room first . . . just in case Mr. Barnett ain't decent or somethin' the like."

"Of course," Savannah agreed.

"Meanwhile, I'll go on out to check on Trenner's horse again," Bill remarked. "That poor animal looked near as worn out as his owner did last night when I put him in the barn. I best make sure he's farin' well before I head to town to telegram ol' Colbalt about his missin' cowhand."

"Be careful, Bill," Lottie said as worry puckered her pretty brows. "The sun's out now, but you never do know when this weather's gonna turn mean."

"I'll be careful, darlin'," Bill said, rising from his chair as he dabbed at his mouth with a napkin. "And I'll be back quick as a wink."

Lottie smiled, returning Bill's kiss as he placed a token of his promise to be safe and return quickly to her lips.

"Come on, Savannah!" Everett whined. "That poor cowboy is probably starved dead by now!"

"I certainly hope not," Savannah teased her brother.

"I agree with Everett," Sadie commented. Then winking at Savannah, she added, "I mean . . . if you must, you must."

Amelia giggled, and Savannah tried to keep a straight face as she thought about the conversation she and her two stepsisters had shared the night before about Trenner Barnett.

"What's so funny?" Everett asked as Savannah followed him the short distance down the hall toward the room where Trenner was convalescing.

"Oh, nothin'," Savannah assured him. "Nothin' little boys would be interested in, anyway."

"Oh, I see," Everett said, rolling his eyes. "Cookin' and doilies and lace . . . things like that?"

"Pretty much," Savannah answered.

Savannah and Everett paused just outside the closed door of Everett's bedroom.

"Reckon we oughta knock first?" Everett asked in a whisper.

"Oh, surely we should," Savannah agreed.

Everett put his ear to the door a moment. "I don't hear no snorin'." His eyes widened a bit then, and he added, "But what if he's usin' the bucket? You know, doin' his business in there right now? It wouldn't be proper to walk in on him, now would it?"

"No! Indeed not!" Savannah exclaimed in a whisper. "And that's why we better knock first."

"All right," Everett said, straightening his posture. "I'll knock. But if he says for us to come in, you best hang back a second or two . . . just in case he's usin' the bucket, all right?"

"Good idea," Savannah agreed, trying not to giggle. The look on Everett's face was that of anticipating embarrassment—and it was adorable.

Inhaling a deep breath, Everett raised his little fist and knocked firmly on the door.

"Yep?" came the deep voice from the other side.

"Uh . . . we got your breakfast out here, Mr. Barnett," Everett almost shouted. "You want that we should bring it in now? Or are you usin' the bucket?"

"Everett, for Pete's sake! Don't ask him if he's usin' the bucket!" Savannah scolded through her barely restrained laughter.

But Everett shrugged and said, "Better safe than sorry, Savannah."

Savannah heard the chuckling emanating from inside Everett's room then.

"Come on in, boy," Trenner called, amusement still apparent in his voice. "It's safe enough."

None too slowly, Everett opened the door to his bedroom.

"We brung you some breakfast, Mr. Barnett,"

Everett announced as he stepped into the room, motioning for Savannah to follow him. "Eggs, bacon, and biscuits too," Everett gleefully announced.

Savannah's eyes widened as Trenner Barnett sat up, raking a hand back through his tousled hair. Blushing as she studied him a moment sitting upright in the bed, the blankets and sheets at his waist and his bare torso exposed, she wondered how on earth it was possible he could look any more astonishingly attractive than he had even the night before—but he did.

"Sounds like heaven," Trenner said, smiling at Everett and then at Savannah.

"Excuse me for askin', mister," Everett began as Savannah made her way to the bedside, "but you look like you've been slung at and hit! Don't you feel no better at all?"

"Everett!" Savannah quietly scolded as she set the tray on the small table next to the bed.

But Trenner chuckled. "Well, I *feel* like I've been slung at and hit," he admitted. "So I reckon I should look the part." He smiled at Everett, reaching and tousling the boy's straw hair. "I'm all right though. Just achin' from the bullets that went through me and still feelin' a bit too warm."

Everett frowned, reached out, and placed his small hand to Trenner's forehead.

"He's burnin' up, Savannah," Everett said. "You best feel for yourself," he added, taking

Savannah's hand and directing her to place it on Trenner's forehead.

Savannah wasn't sure if it were Trenner's fever or the fact that she was touching him that caused her flush from head to toe. Either way, she could determine that Trenner's fever had not subsided. If anything, it was worse.

"You best fetch Mama, Everett," she said calmly—though she hadn't known worry the depth that was rising in her for a very long time.

Trenner gazed up into the soft green eyes of Bill Dickerson's stepdaughter. Dang, if she wasn't the prettiest little filly he'd ever seen! Her skin was flawless—looked as if it would feel like velvet if he were to reach out and touch her cheek. Her lips were a perfectly tempting pink, and the way her thick, dark eyelashes fluttered when she blinked made Trenner's stomach knot up with admiration—and desire.

"I will!" Everett assured his sister as he raced from the room.

Trenner chuckled, touched by the boy's concern.

"He's a tenderhearted little feller, ain't he?" he asked.

"Yes, he is," the pretty girl that had brought his breakfast answered.

"Well, Miss Savannah," Trenner began, "if I really am still a bit under the weather, I'm sure it ain't nothin' this fine breakfast can't fix up."

Tossing the bedding aside, Trenner swung his legs off the side of the bed and snitched a piece of bacon from the plate of food Savannah had brought.

The girl's pretty face instantly turned red as a beet, and she glanced away quickly.

"Sorry 'bout that," Trenner said, tugging at the bedsheet to cover his lap. "I guess I'm too used to a bunkhouse full of cowhands runnin' around in their underwear. I ain't accustomed to ladies bein' in the room with me when I've been asleep."

"Oh, it's fine," Savannah said.

But Trenner grinned, amused as he noted the way the girl made sure her gaze stayed directly on his face.

"I don't know how I'm ever gonna repay your daddy and mama for takin' me in like this," Trenner said. "As soon as I'm up and about this mornin', I'll just head out to the bunkhouse where I belong."

"You're still feverish, Mr. Barnett," Savannah reminded him. "That drafty old bunkhouse is no place for a man in your condition."

"Bill Dickerson's bunkhouse is the best built bunkhouse I ever had the honor to stay in," Trenner offered, however. "The warmest winters I ever spent were the ones I spent workin' for him. So I'll be just fine out there."

• • •

"Over my dead body," Lottie said as she entered the room with Everett hot on her heels. "I won't have you convalescin' anywhere but in here—and for more reasons than just your own well-bein'. You wouldn't want to give the other boys fever now, would you, Mr. Barnett?"

"No, ma'am," Trenner said, glancing at Savannah with a wink of amusement for the sake of her mother's dramatics.

Savannah smiled—both because Trenner had winked at her and because her mother was wise enough to insist he convalesce in the house.

"Still, I wouldn't want to share my fever with your daughters, Everett here, or you and Mr. Dickerson for that matter, ma'am," Trenner said. "I'm sure I'll be fine and—"

"Eat your breakfast and then rest, Mr. Barnett," Lottie interrupted, however. Striding to where he sat, she placed one of her hands to his forehead.

Savannah frowned when her mother exhaled a concerned sigh.

"You're too warm for my likin'," her mother said. "How's your chest feelin'? Are you coughin' even just a little?"

"No, ma'am," Trenner answered. "I'm sure it'll pass here quick enough."

"Well, let's hope so," Lottie said, smiling with compassion. Still looking at Trenner, she added,

"Savannah, why don't you girls draw up a bath out in the summer kitchen for Mr. Barnett here? That'll do him wonders to feelin' better. But have Everett build a fire out there and warm it up a piece first, all right?"

"Of course, Mama," Savannah said. Looking to Everett, she whispered, "You heard Mama. Run along and build a fire out in the summer kitchen, all right?"

Everett smiled and nodded, obviously happy to do anything that might help Trenner be more comfortable. Savannah thought it wonderful that Everett was so concerned over the sick cowboy. She'd never seen him so helpful and willing before.

"Oh, Mrs. Dickerson, it's not necessary to put your young ladies to so much trouble. Please don't," Trenner began.

"We're happy to do it," Savannah interrupted, however. "You'll feel much better after a long soak in a warm tub, Mr. Barnett."

Trenner's handsome brow puckered into a frown. "But it don't make no sense to bathe up and then slip right back into dirty clothin', Miss Savannah. I'd best just skip the tub."

"Oh, I'm sure we can find some long johns that'll fit you, Mr. Barnett," Lottie assured the man. "And I'll wash up your jeans and shirt, patch them a bit, and you'll feel as shiny as a new pressed penny. Don't you worry."

Again Trenner raked one hand back through his tousled hair. Savannah could plainly see that the man wasn't at all comfortable being fussed over or inconveniencing others.

"But I haven't even seen to my horse yet or anythin'," he mumbled. Savannah could see worry and anxiety beginning to mingle with his already bruised pride.

"Oh, Bill saw to your horse and rig last night, and again this mornin' on his way to town to send a telegram to your employer," Lottie explained. "So you just relax and let us womenfolk take care of you until you're feelin' better."

It was a statement—a command—not a request.

Trenner shook his head, grinned up at Savannah, swiped another piece of bacon from the plate on the bed table, and sighed with resignation. "If you say so, ma'am."

Savannah smiled, knowing that it was purely the fact that her mother and Bill had done so much for Trenner already that kept him from leaping out of bed and marching out of the house. He was well mannered. Furthermore, he was able and willing to swallow his pride in order to please those who had inconvenienced themselves for his sake. It was apparent that Trenner Barnett was a man to be admired for his good character, as well as his good looks.

"I do say so," Lottie said, smiling. "Now you eat up that breakfast and then take a long soak. We'll change your bandages once you're finished, all right?"

"Yes, ma'am," Trenner agreed.

"I'll get Sadie and Amelia started on heatin' some water," Lottie said. "Why don't you give Mr. Barnett some company with his breakfast, Savannah?"

"I'd be happy to," Savannah said—and she *would* be.

Taking a small chair from its place in one corner of the room, Savannah placed it next to the bed. Stirring the coals in the hearth, she added one small log before sitting down.

"We don't want it gettin' too cold in here for you," she said, clasping her hands in her lap as she faced the handsome cowboy.

"Thank you," Trenner said as he took his breakfast plate from the tray on the night table and placed it on his lap. Using the fork Savannah's mother provided, he took his first bite of eggs, sighing with satisfaction as he chewed.

"Well, at least you've got an appetite," Savannah said. "That's as good a sign as any that you're on the mend."

"I surely hope so," Trenner said. "I can't take too much more of this pamperin'. I'll turn soft."

Savannah smiled as she watched him eat for a moment. Then, for the sake of making sure he didn't think she was just some crazy woman who enjoyed staring at him—although she did enjoy staring at him—she offered, "So I guess those rustlers you were chasin' are long gone now, hmmm?"

Trenner frowned as he continued to eat his breakfast. "Oh, there's no doubt of that," he agreed. "I'll be lucky if Mr. Colbalt even lets me finish out winterin' at his place after lettin' them cattle get taken."

It was Savannah's turn to frown. "But . . . but it wasn't your fault," she reminded him.

"Colbalt won't see it that way," Trenner said. He shook his head. "That man is ornery if anybody ever was. And he chooses to blame anybody for anything, even if it don't make a lick of sense. I wasn't even workin' last night. I was comin' back from town the back way around things when I seen them men cut out the cattle. But ol' Colbalt . . . he won't see reason anywhere."

Wanting to lighten the subject for the sake of Trenner's well-being, Savannah asked, "Why did you leave here? I mean, bein' that you used to cowboy for Bill . . . why didn't you just stay on? I'm sure he's much kinder to work for than this Mr. Colbalt."

"Oh, Bill Dickerson is the best man I've ever cowboyed for," Trenner assured her firmly. He shrugged. "But I got the chance to go on this long drive up to Wyomin' a few years back, and I went—even though Bill told me I'd regret it . . . which I did. In fact, it was miserable and took me so long to get back down this way, I knew Bill wouldn't be hirin'. So I just signed on with Colbalt when he asked."

"Well, my daddy was a rancher too, and there's always room for a fine cowboy like yourself," Savannah said.

Trenner paused in eating, staring at Savannah a moment. Finally, he said, "How do you know I'm a fine cowboy? Maybe I'm a lazy, yeller good-for-nothin'."

Savannah smiled and shook her head. "I heard what Bill said—that he'd rather have one of you than five other cowboys. He would've hired you back, no questions asked."

Again Trenner shrugged, and Savannah couldn't help but notice, once more, how broad his shoulders were—his broad, muscular shoulders attached to his broad, muscular chest and long, muscular arms.

"I suppose I had my tail between my legs a bit—you know, too proud to come beggin' for a place back here," Trenner admitted, "especially after Bill had warned me I ought not go in the first place."

"Pride goeth before the fall, is it?" Savannah playfully asked.

Trenner chuckled, "Yes, ma'am. Indeed it does."

Savannah kept smiling, awed by how quickly

Trenner finished the plate of food she'd brought to him.

"And now, Miss Savannah," he began as he returned the plate and fork to the tray on the side table and stood up, "if you wouldn't mind leadin' me to my boots and coat, I think it's about time I took a stroll out to the hitchin' post."

Savannah giggled. After all, he looked so weak and groggy. Oh, certainly he was tall, beautiful, and his mere presence looming before her caused butterflies to rise in her stomach and goose bumps to prickle her arms and legs. Still, he looked so much like a mischievous boy standing there in his long underwear with his hair still tousled.

"Mama will skin me alive if I let you go out in this cold," Savannah explained.

"Well, Miss Savannah," Trenner said, reaching down and taking both of her hands in his and pulling her to her feet, "I sure as hell ain't gonna use that bucket under the bed. It's one thing to let you and your mama mollycoddle me where food, injuries, and fever are concerned . . . but I won't have no one dumpin' a bucket after me."

His hands were so warm where they held hers—hot even. And although she knew it was his fever she was sensing in his touch, Savannah relished it a moment longer than she should've.

"All right," she agreed at last. "But you're takin' the consequences from Mama all on yourself."

"Of course," Trenner said, still holding her hands—still standing in front of her, gazing down into her eyes and smiling at her.

"Then I'll fetch your coat and boots and start you toward the privy," Savannah said. "But if you get caught . . ."

"I won't say a word," Trenner assured her. "Not one word."

"Very well. Wait here," Savannah whispered.

As she hurried out of Everett's bedroom, she could hear her mother, Sadie, and Amelia talking in the summer kitchen at the back of the house. Quickly she fetched Trenner's coat, hat, and boots, returning to the bedroom and offering them to him.

"You best be quick if you don't want to get caught," she whispered.

"Yes, ma'am," Trenner said, plopping his hat haphazardly onto his head and then pulling on his coat and boots.

Savannah gasped when the handsome cowboy leaned over, kissing her quickly on one cheek and in a lowered voice saying, "Buckets under the bed are for little boys and old men. I thank you for helpin' me escape it, Miss Savannah."

Breathless and nearly dizzy from the euphoric feel of his lips to her cheek—no matter how brief—Savannah nodded and barely managed to whisper, "Y-you best head out the kitchen side door. You'll find the privy out back of the house."

"Thank you, ma'am," Trenner said, touching the brim of his hat as he smiled at Savannah. "I'll be back before anybody else knows I'm gone."

Savannah nodded, still too overwhelmed with near delirium to speak anything further.

Once Trenner had disappeared into the hallway, Savannah collapsed on her seat on the bed. Placing a hand to her cheek where he'd kissed her, she could've sworn she could still feel his kiss there—and it was heavenly!

"So? What did you do then, mister?" Everett asked as he poured another kettle of hot water into the tub.

"I hauled off and give him what for with my fists and elbows and everything else about me," Trenner answered. "The varmint didn't deserve no mercy, not after what he'd done." Trenner shook his head. "You don't ever stand by and let a man talk that way to a lady, boy . . . not ever."

Everett smiled. The more time he spent in the company of Trenner Barnett, the more he knew, without a doubt, that the Lord had sent the cowboy for Savannah for Christmas.

"Did you black up both his eyes, Trenner?" Everett asked with excitement.

"And then some," Trenner admitted. The cowboy frowned then, adding, "Though don't go thinkin' I'm encouragin' you to go fightin' and all, Everett."

"Oh, I know you ain't," Everett assured him.

Trenner nodded. "But when it comes to defendin' a lady . . . fists a-flyin' is sometimes the only way to put a rat in his place, do you know what I mean?"

"I do," Everett affirmed. The boy stuck his finger into the tub water. "Not too hot. Good thing, else Mama would have my hide. She says I can't get your water too hot, bein' as you're already with fever."

"She's a wise woman, your mama," Trenner stated.

Everett smiled. "Yep. Mama's as wise as Savannah is pretty. Don't you agree?"

Trenner grinned. The poor kid couldn't hide his conniving to save the world.

"I would agree. I surely would," Trenner admitted.

He began to worry, however. Of course, Trenner had been worried from the moment young Everett told him that Trenner Barnett was an answer to a prayer. If there was one thing Trenner knew, it was that *he* certainly wasn't an answer to any prayer. And beyond that fact, he was deeply worried about the disappointment Everett would experience when Trenner did get back on his feet and left for good—and alone.

"Uh . . . Everett?" Trenner began. It was going

to be hard to rattle the boy's faith, but Trenner knew it was better done sooner than later.

"Yes, sir?" Everett said, smiling at Trenner with joyous anticipation.

"Uh, you know that I can't just waltz in one night and . . . well . . . and win over your sister, or whatever it is you're expectin'," Trenner began. "Things just don't work that way in life. Do you know what I'm sayin'?"

But Everett just laughed—literally laughed.

"But don't you see, Mr. Barnett? You already have!" he said. "Why, I ain't seen Savannah this bright-eyed and bushy-tailed in so long . . . *ever* maybe! And if you're worried that you won't like her back, just give it a day or two." The boy shrugged. "After all, it's still thirteen more days 'til Christmas Eve. That's plenty of time for you to see how beautiful Savannah is."

"Oh, I ain't sayin' she ain't beautiful," Trenner admitted. "I'm just sayin' . . . well, things just don't work out that way. I'm a cowboy, and cowboys . . . well, we don't have nothin' to offer a fine woman like your sister."

Everett smiled at Trenner—sympathetically smiled at Trenner. Placing a hand on Trenner's shoulder, Everett said, "You don't know nothin' about women, do you, Mr. Barnett? Nothin' at all."

"I . . . uh . . . I . . ." Trenner stammered. The boy was nothing if not steadfast in his faith and belief that God had sent Trenner for the sake of his sister.

"You got everything Savannah needs," Everett assured him. "I seen the way her eyes lit up when you walked in last night . . . how all blushy and nervous she gets whenever you look at her. Besides, you're a good man, a hard-workin' man, and I heard Daddy tell Mama last night—after you had gone to sleep and all—I heard him tell her that he couldn't wish nothin' better for any of his girls than lassoin' a man the likes of you. So you see? You just have to give it a bit of time, a couple of days. Then you'll see."

Trenner exhaled a heavy sigh of discouragement and forfeit. The truth was, he didn't feel altogether well. The soak had helped, but he still felt weak, thirsty, and his head was pounding in rhythm with the aches in his arm and leg where Mrs. Dickerson had stitched him up the night before.

"Everett," he mumbled, "I just don't want you to be disappointed if . . . well, when I leave here . . . by myself."

Again Everett patted Trenner on one shoulder.

"What's say we get you out of the tub and back to bed," Everett said.

Trenner grinned, thinking the boy had his mother's gift of healing—and bossiness.

"Then we can talk about it later. Does that sound all right?" the boy asked.

"Fine," Trenner conceded. He didn't have any fight in him at all—not even enough gumption to stand up to a willful child.

"Okeydokey then, here's you a towel," Everett said, retrieving a towel from a hook on one wall of the summer kitchen. "You get dried off, and I'll see if Mama's found you some fresh long johns." Everett studied Trenner for a moment and then added, "I don't see you squeezin' into a pair of Daddy's though." He shrugged, adding, "But miracles do happen." Everett winked at Trenner and whispered, "Miracles *do* happen, Mr. Barnett—especially 'round Christmas." Everett handed Trenner the towel and with one final smile of reassurance said, "You dry off, and I'll be right back with a pair of clean socks and some underwear of some kind."

The boy hurried off into the house, and Trenner—too tired and weak to argue—stood up out of the tub and began drying off. He was discomfited by his own weakness. Why, the way he felt right then, he wondered if he'd ever be able to bloody the nose of any man disrespecting a lady ever again.

"Savannah!" Everett called into his room, where Savannah was straightening the bed in preparation for the family guest to rest further. "Come quick! Mr. Barnett ain't feelin' too well!"

Savannah's heart leapt in her chest, leapt with

fear and trepidation. In fact, she was so overwhelmed with dread—with anxiety over Trenner Barnett's well-being—that she didn't even pause to think of calling for her mother but rather hurried down the hall after Everett toward the summer kitchen.

"He's in here, Savannah!" Everett prodded. Going to stand behind her, Everett shoved Savannah hard from behind just as she stepped into the summer kitchen to see Trenner Barnett standing next to the tub with only a towel wrapped around his waist for covering.

"See him? I think his fever's worse!" Everett exclaimed, shoving Savannah again. This time her brother shoved her hard enough to propel her forward with such force that she completely lost her footing.

A light squeal of astonishment escaped Savannah's throat as she stumbled forward and against the bare-chested Trenner Barnett.

"You all right there, Miss—?" the cowboy began to ask. But clearly the man wasn't up to his full strength—because before Savannah had time to even blink, Trenner Barnett slipped on the summer kitchen floor, wrapping his arms tightly around her as he fell backward.

Savannah closed her eyes as the water splashed onto her face—opened them a moment later, however, to find herself lying against Trenner Barnett as he once more sat in the tub.

"Oh! Oh! Oh my!" Savannah exclaimed, breathless as she placed her hands on Trenner's chest to support herself.

Instantly Trenner's gaze met hers; his dark, alluring gaze met hers, and she couldn't breathe, nor move.

Slowly a grin of delight spread across his handsome face. "I've never bathed up with a lady before," he said in a low, rather provocative voice.

"I-I . . . I'm so sorry," Savannah stammered.

"Oh, please don't apologize, Miss Savannah," Trenner flirted.

Yes! He was flirting with her, and Savannah didn't know whether to slap him for being so crude or kiss him for being so playful!

It was Everett's unbridled laughter that finally snapped Savannah to attention once more.

"Everett Ambrose!" Savannah scolded, still sitting in the tub on Trenner Barnett's lap. "You did that on purpose! I know you did!"

"Of course I did it on purpose, Savannah! You ninny!" Everett unashamedly confessed. "And it's worth any lecture or extra chorin' I get from Mama or Bill . . . 'cause you two sittin' there in that tub . . ." Everett couldn't finish his sentence for the fact that he was doubled over slapping one knee as he tried to catch his breath while nearly busting a gut with laughter.

By now Trenner Barnett was beginning to

laugh as well, and when Savannah looked back to him—saw the merriment in his dark eyes, the dazzling flash of his perfect smile—she felt wild giggles rising up in her own throat.

"I'm so very sorry, Mr. Barnett," Savannah laughed as she stood up and stepped out of the tub, slopping water everywhere. "I'm . . . I'm sure Everett will get a tongue-thrashin' the likes he's never known when Mama finds out about this!"

"Why does she have to find out?" Trenner asked through his own laughter.

At Trenner's suggestion that news of the incident didn't need to be shared, Everett's and Savannah's laughter abruptly stopped.

"What?" Everett asked. "You mean . . . you mean you ain't gonna tell on me?"

Trenner shook his head as he combed his fingers back through his wet hair. "I don't see why I'd need to."

Savannah watched as Trenner began to pull himself up out of the tub—felt her eyebrows arch as he paused, looked down, and then asked, "Everett? You wouldn't happen to have a dry towel handy, now would you? This one's at the bottom of the tub and won't do much good for dryin' off or coverin' up now."

"What is all the commotion?" Sadie asked as she stepped into the room.

"Oh, my stars and garters!" Amelia gasped,

covering her mouth as she surveyed the scene before her.

"Savannah? What on earth?" Sadie inquired in a whisper, her eyes locked on where Trenner Barnett sat in the tub.

"Trenner ain't gonna rat on me to Mama and Daddy," Everett began babbling. "So if you two don't say nothin', then nobody will get in trouble for me pushin' Savannah into the bath with Mr. Barnett here."

"What?" Sadie and Amelia exclaimed, their eyes widening to the size of the harvest moon.

"I stumbled forward and knocked Mr. Barnett back into the tub and . . . and . . ." Savannah stammered, desperate to explain.

"And tumbled right in with him?" Amelia squeaked.

"Well . . . well, yes. But he was wearin' a towel around him," Savannah pointed out. Blushing, she added, "At least he was when we went in."

Savannah held her breath, terrified of what her new sisters would think of her—of what they would tell her mother and Bill.

All at once, however, both Sadie and Amelia burst into giggling.

"Well, we best get this mess cleaned up before Lottie gets back from the henhouse or Daddy gets back from town, that's for sure!" Sadie suggested.

"Here, Savannah," Amelia said, taking a towel from a hook on the wall and tossing it to her.

"Hurry up and go change. We'll clean up in here. Now go! Before we're all caught!"

Everett dashed to where the towels were kept, pulling a dry towel off the wall and taking it to Trenner. "Dry off, Mr. Barnett . . . for good this time."

"Hurry, Everett," Sadie instructed. "Help me sop up this water. In fact, let's just start emptyin' the tub with the bucket. That way it'll just look like we slopped water while we were throwin' out the bathwater."

As Savannah wrapped the towel around her, she paused to look at Trenner Barnett once more before heading to her room to change.

He smiled and winked at her, and she bit her lip with delight in knowing he'd enjoyed their ridiculous little moment of awkward closeness as much as she had.

"You be sure and dry off real good, mister," Everett instructed as he took Trenner's hand and pulled him along down the hall toward his bedroom. "You've already got a fever, and I don't want you catchin' cold too."

Trenner chuckled as the boy led him into the bedroom.

"There's your underwear and some clean socks. Mama still dryin' your shirt and trousers by the fire in the parlor. But you'll be warm enough as long as I keep your fire stoked in here."

Everett went to the hearth and immediately began stirring the coals to warm the room.

As he pulled on a pair of long underwear that were a little tight but comfortable enough, Trenner shook his head and smiled.

"Well, I'll give you this, Everett," he began. "You ain't one to fiddle around. Just pushed your sister right in the bath with me to get things rollin', huh?"

"Well, somebody had to start the wagon rollin'," Everett said, smiling at Trenner.

Trenner nodded. "I guess so," he chuckled. "The amazin' part about it . . . was that she didn't even seem the least bit perturbed."

"Savannah's a lot of fun," Everett confirmed. "She's just had a lot of sadness in her life these past few years, so sometimes a body has to draw her out. But she hardly ever gets mad about anything. It's one of the things you'll like most about her."

"Is it now?" Trenner asked, shaking his head in amused disbelief.

The boy was persistent, Trenner would give him that.

But then, as he sat down on the bed once more feeling groggy, overheated, and weak, an image of Savannah staring down at him from her position in the bathtub over him leapt to the forefront of his mind. Those leaf-green eyes of hers were bewitching in that moment; all of her was bewitching in that moment. And as Trenner thought about it all a little longer, he realized that it wasn't in just that moment that Savannah had bewitched him. It was from the instant their eyes had met the night before—when he'd first entered the house and Bill had introduced the new members of his family to him.

Yet it was, all of it, nonsense—pure nonsense. A man didn't just walk into a house one night and meet the woman he'd spent his adult life looking for. Things didn't work that way.

And then Everett said, "Why don't you climb on into bed while I fetch you a fresh glass of water and some bread and jam? Then you can sleep for a while. All right, Mr. Barnett?"

"Sounds fine," Trenner mumbled as he studied Everett.

As Everett took off down the hall, Trenner wondered—could it be true? Could the boy's prayer be what brought Trenner back to Bill Dickerson's place? Was he meant for Savannah and Savannah for him?

Shaking his head at the preposterous musings of his fevered mind, Trenner did crawl into bed. Exhaling a heavy sigh of fatigue, he closed his eyes. Yet all he could envision was Savannah—her smile, her leaf-green eyes, and her berry-colored lips. He felt his mouth flood with the warmth of desire as he continued to think of

Savannah—of her kindness, her beauty, and her sense of humor.

All at once, the memory of her expression when she'd opened her eyes in the summer kitchen to find herself in the tub with Trenner flashed into his mind—and he couldn't keep from laughing out loud. Furthermore, scandalous as it had been, she'd been pleased when he'd teased her about never having bathed with a lady before—and he liked that she'd been pleased. It revealed something to Trenner about her: it revealed that maybe Everett was right, that maybe Savannah had taken to Trenner a bit already.

CHAPTER FOUR

"Well, I'll tell you one thing," Bill began as he sat at the supper table across from Trenner. "I ain't a bit surprised. Colbalt blames somebody else for everything."

Savannah watched Trenner closely. It was apparent his first reaction to the news that Mr. Colbalt didn't want him returning to his ranch—the news that he was blaming Trenner for fifteen head of his cattle being taken and the reality that they would never be retrieved—was anger.

"I figured he'd let me go for it," Trenner mumbled, still frowning. "I had a bad feelin' about winterin' at his place from the beginning." He shrugged. "But I didn't have any other irons in the fire. So that's where I stayed."

"Well, you've got a place in my bunkhouse for as long as you like," Bill said. Smiling, he tore the telegram from Walt Colbalt to pieces, stood up, strode to the cookstove, opened the fire door, and tossed it into the flames. "I've been wishin' you'd stayed on with me since the day you left, boy," Bill continued. "And come spring . . . well,

I could sure use a good hand like you. You know that."

"I appreciate your charity, Mr. Dickerson—" Trenner began.

"It ain't charity, Trenner," Bill interrupted, however. "You know that."

Everett hopped up out of his own chair, hurried to where Trenner sat, patted him on one shoulder, and said, "You see, mister? Things are workin' out just like they're supposed to. I knew they would."

Savannah was curious as to why Trenner seemed a bit unsettled as he looked to Everett, seemed to force a reassuring smile, and said, "We'll have to see, Everett. We'll have to see."

"Well, I'll tell you one thing, Trenner Barnett," Bill began with a smile. "Sometimes when things look the worst ahead of ya, it's just because they're about to get better. So let me hire you on for the winter to help the other hands with things, and then when spring arrives, I can promise you you'll be busier than a one-eyed cat watchin' two mouse holes!"

Trenner smiled, amused by Bill's phrasing.

"Please do stay, Mr. Barnett," Lottie added then. "Bill really can use your help 'round the ranch."

"And besides," Amelia piped up, "you know us already. And Sadie is sweet on Clay Picket now, so she won't be stickin' to your boot heel anymore."

"Amelia!" Sadie exclaimed, blushing crimson.

Everyone at the table snickered a little at Amelia's embarrassing her older sister—everyone but Sadie, of course.

"I really could use your help, Trenner," Bill reiterated.

Trenner inhaled a deep breath, and Savannah could see his jaw clench with swallowing his pride.

"I'd be a fool not to come to work for you, Mr. Dickerson," Trenner began. "But I would ask that Mrs. Dickerson allow me to stay out in the bunkhouse with the other hands. I don't want any special treatment if I'm on your pay, sir."

Bill nodded and looked to Lottie. "Sounds good to me. What do you say, Lottie?"

Savannah held her breath—silently prayed that her mother would agree to let Trenner convalesce out in the bunkhouse—for she wanted nothing more in all the world than for the handsome cowboy to stay on and work for her stepfather.

Lottie smiled with understanding, reached out, and placed a maternal hand over Trenner's where it rested on the table beside his supper plate. For his part, Everett still stood next to Trenner, leaning on the cowboy's shoulder as if he'd known the man his entire life.

"I'll make you a deal, Mr. Barnett," Lottie began. "You stay in here, in the house, until that fever you've got is gone . . . completely gone.

Then I'd be grateful if you would indeed stay on to work for Bill." Lottie nodded, adding, "And I promise that as soon as that fever has left you, you can head on out to that drafty old bunkhouse and be as uncomfortable as you like for the rest of the winter, okeydokey?"

Trenner exhaled a heavy sigh of relief, smiled, and said, "Agreed. I'll keep to the house a day or so, per your instructions, ma'am. But then I'll head on out to the bunkhouse with the others." Trenner stretched one strong, callused hand across the table toward Bill.

"Thank you, son," Bill said, shaking Trenner's hand. "I can't tell you how relieved I'll be to have you back. These other boys are like herdin' cats sometimes, you know?"

"I do," Trenner agreed.

Savannah's heart swelled inside her. Trenner Barnett would be staying on to work for Bill! She exchanged glances of gladness and mischief with Sadie and Amelia—both of whom had kept entirely mum about what had gone on in the summer kitchen earlier in the day.

For her part, butterflies took flight in Savannah's stomach every time she thought back on the incident—thought back on how mesmerizing Trenner's gaze had been when he'd smiled at her and said, *I've never bathed up with a lady before.* Oh, it was entirely inappropriate! In fact, Savannah knew she should've slapped him rather than felt giddy about it. But she hadn't—and she had no regret about not doing so.

Trenner glanced to her from his place across the table, grinning at her. Savannah wondered for a moment if maybe one reason he'd agreed to stay on and work for Bill was because of her. Of course, she knew that was a preposterous notion. But she decided to pretend it was true—at least for a little while.

"Well, you got a lot more color in your face than you did this mornin'," Lottie said. "I really do think you're on the mend. Are those bullet holes botherin' you at all?"

Trenner rotated his left elbow a bit, shook his head, and answered, "Nope. Not hardly at all."

Lottie smiled and nodded with approval. "Oh, good. I'm glad to hear it. No doubt that soak in the tub you had this mornin' helped the soreness subside a bit."

Amelia and Sadie bit their lips to keep from giggling as Trenner looked directly at Savannah, smiled, and said, "Oh yes, ma'am. That bath did wonders for me . . . wonders indeed."

Savannah blushed so deeply that Everett asked, frowning, "You all right, Savannah? Are ya too hot or somethin'?"

"N-no, I'm fine," Savannah managed.

"Well, I'm glad you're feelin' better, Mr. Barnett," Lottie sighed. "And I'm guessin' you'll sleep better tonight and wake bright-eyed and bushy-tailed first thing in the mornin'."

"Yes, ma'am, I'm sure I will," Trenner said, still grinning at Savannah.

Savannah felt as if she might simply burst apart! He was staring at her so intently, she imagined he could tell exactly what she was thinking. And she was thinking that she was so wildly attracted to him—found him so intriguing—that she never, ever wanted him to be out of her sight again!

Sadie and Amelia were struggling greatly in attempting to keep from rupturing into giggles, and Everett even let one snicker slip.

Bill's eyes narrowed as he looked at each of his children in turn. "I'll tell you one thing, Lottie," he began. "There's somethin' goin' on in the minds of our brood here . . . somethin' we ain't aware of."

"Indeed," Lottie agreed. Her attention settled exactly on Everett. Then she asked, "Everett? Have you been into mischief again?"

Everett gulped, plastered an awkward smile on his face, and answered, "Well, yes, I have, Mama. After all, it *is* Christmas, and I've got gifts I'm workin' on just like everybody else."

"Is that so?" Lottie asked with suspicion.

"Yes, Mama," Everett said. He gulped guiltily, however.

Savannah smiled when Trenner came to her brother's rescue. "I can attest to that, Mrs.

Dickerson," Trenner said. "Everett here even let me in on what he's up to. So I can tell you that he is bein' truthful. He is workin' on Christmas gifts and such."

Savannah looked to her mother, relieved to see that she indeed looked satisfied. If Trenner said Everett was about working on gifts, then apparently Lottie was willing to take the cowboy at his word.

"All right then," Lottie said. Nevertheless, she looked to Bill, adding, "Though I'm inclined to agree with your daddy. I smell more mischief about than just keepin' gifts a secret."

"Here, let me take your plate, Mama," Savannah said, nearly leaping from her chair. "Let's clear the table, and then we can all settle in the parlor and enjoy the tree."

"I do have to mention," Trenner began as Savannah removed her mother's plate from the table, "that I've never seen a Christmas tree brung into the house so early before. Most folks, don't they wait 'til right before . . . or even Christmas Eve?"

Lottie smiled proudly and answered, "Well, Bill and I both feel that a Christmas tree is meant to be enjoyed much longer than just one or two nights. After all, we all should be thinkin' about our Savior and his birth every day of the year, not just at Christmastime. So Bill thought that if we cut our tree early and stuck the trunk down in a bucket, it would stay fresh enough for us to enjoy it for a few weeks instead of a few days."

Trenner nodded. "It's a good idea. And might I add that yours is one of the most beautiful Christmas trees I've ever seen? Because it certainly is."

"I helped gather the berries!" Everett interjected.

Trenner smiled, reaching up to tousle Everett's head of straw. "And them berries really do make it so much more festive, don't they?"

Everett smiled and nodded. "That's what Mama said."

Savannah exhaled the breath she'd been holding ever since Bill pointed out that he thought some sort of mischief was about. Each bringing other supper plates from the table to the sink, Amelia and Sadie both looked at Savannah with knowing expressions.

"That was unsettlin'," Amelia whispered.

"I'll say!" Sadie whispered in agreement. "Just imagine if Lottie would've found out you'd been in the tub with that man, Savannah!"

"I know!" Savannah softly replied. "No doubt she would've called down the lightning from heaven to strike me where I stand!"

"More secrets, girls?" Bill chuckled.

"Well, it *is* Christmastime," Savannah said.

"And that's part of the fun," Sadie offered. "Don't you agree, Daddy?"

"Mmm hmmm," Bill answered.

Savannah glanced over her shoulder to see Bill smiling at her. He winked—as if to say, *I ain't as blind as you think I am*—and then turned back to the conversation going on at the table.

The three young women at the sink exchanged impish grins, and Savannah felt her heart warm all the more toward her two new sisters. After all, if they were willing to help hide the scandalous goings-on that had taken place in the summer kitchen between her and Trenner Barnett, then Savannah felt she could trust them with anything!

"Well, I for one have never witnessed such a thing in all my life!" Amelia quietly exclaimed as Savannah, Sadie, and Amelia lay in their beds later that night.

"And with your life bein' oh-so-long, I suppose that's unusual?" Sadie teased. "That you've never seen a woman fall into a bathtub with a man?" Sadie laughed, adding, "Of course you've never seen it! Not one of us has! At least before today."

"I should've slapped him," Savannah offered. Yet still smiling, she added, "But I didn't want to . . . not at all!"

"You should've kissed him!" Sadie suggested. "I know I would've!"

As Amelia laughed wholeheartedly, Savannah gasped, "Oh my heavens, no! He would've thought I was a scarlet woman for certain!"

"So you're sayin' that you thought about it?" Sadie asked in a very quiet whisper.

Savannah knew the moment was upon her. Just over the course of one day, she'd managed to draw closer to Sadie and Amelia than in all the months before combined. She wanted sisters—real sisters—sisters that she could trust, confide in, cry to.

And so, very quietly, Savannah admitted, "I absolutely did!"

As Sadie and Amelia broke into giggles of delight, Savannah continued, "I mean, he just makes my heart feel near to burstin'! Every time he looks at me, I feel like I can't breathe! And when I was in the tub with him—when he was starin' me right in the eyes—for a moment, I truly *did* think about kissin' him. Right on the lips too!"

"Oh, I wish you would've!" Amelia exclaimed. "How romantic that would've made it all."

Savannah shook her head. "No. He would've probably hopped outta that tub and run screamin' for the hills."

"Not without a dry towel he wouldn't have," Amelia giggled.

Savannah and Sadie erupted into laughter. And even though all three girls buried their faces in their pillows to try and muffle their amusement, Bill hollered, "All right, girls, it's time to get to sleep. Everett's whinin' 'cause you all are leavin' him out of the fun. So settle down and quit all that gigglin'."

"Yes, Daddy," Sadie and Amelia called.

There was silence for a moment. Then Bill said, "Savannah?"

Being that her heart was so light with merriment and fluttery feelings for Trenner Barnett, Savannah inhaled a breath of courage and called, "Yes, Daddy."

"All right then," Bill said. "You girls sleep tight. I love you, my three angels."

"Love you too, Daddy," Savannah, Sadie, and Amelia chimed in unison.

Savannah had a sudden sense of heightened gladness. She'd finally done it! She'd finally found the courage to call Bill "Daddy" instead of sir, Bill, or just simply avoiding referring to him at all. For so long she'd wanted to think of Bill as more than just the kind man her mother had married. She'd wanted to think of him as a second father. But she'd never been able to get past the guilt—a feeling that she'd be betraying her real father if she did so.

Yet for some reason, in that moment, in that evening—in knowing that Trenner Barnett was in the room across the hall and that he'd be staying on at the ranch—somehow it not only gave Savannah courage but also helped her to feel secure, hopeful, even excited in anticipating her future life. For so long Savannah had carried around secret feelings—worries of never moving forward herself. Certainly her mother had eventually overcome her father's death and managed to find love again. So had Everett. But Savannah had struggled in finding beauty and hope anywhere—and for a very long time.

But not now! Now she felt happier than she had in years. She felt hopeful, silly, and unafraid to love Bill as a second father. Savannah found she owned desire toward Trenner Barnett as well—the desire to flirt with him and be flirted with—to feel his touch the way she had when he'd kissed her cheek. She wanted to gaze into his eyes forever; she wanted to kiss him! It was as if Trenner had somehow managed to unlock her heart.

As Savannah exchanged good night wishes with her sisters, she wondered how in the world she would ever get to sleep that night! Her mind was so alive with questions, hope, possibilities. It would take her hours to fall into a decent slumber. Yet she knew she must try. The next morning would bring chores, cooking, preparations for Christmas, and more glimpses of and glances at Trenner Barnett.

And so Savannah closed her eyes, determined to fall asleep. So many wonderful visions of Trenner Barnett filled her mind, however, that Savannah found she was more even agitated than before! Visions of Trenner as he'd stepped into the house the night before—visions of Trenner stripping off his bloodstained shirt, visions of him eating breakfast, and certainly visions of him as he'd appeared while grinning at her in the bathtub.

When the clock in the parlor struck eleven, indicating to Savannah that she'd been lying in bed wide awake and with only Trenner Barnett on her mind, she knew something had to be done.

Savannah sat up in her bed and looked toward the door. The embers in the hearth of the room she shared with her sisters were barely glowing. But she could see by the warm, low light casting shadows down the hallway that the parlor fire must still be simmering, at least a little. Therefore, she decided that perhaps sitting on the parlor sofa in front of the hearth and reading by lamplight or simply enjoying the beauty of the Christmas tree might be enough of a change to make her sleepy.

Quietly Savannah rose from her bed, pulled on a pair of warm stockings she kept on her night table, put on the rag-robe that lay at the foot of her bed, and silently made her way down the hall to the parlor.

"Ahhh," she sighed as she rather plopped down on the sofa. Tucking her feet beneath her, Savannah gazed at the beautiful Christmas tree. Naturally, being that the only light in the room was the dying embers in the hearth, she couldn't see the tree clearly. Yet the moonlight through the front window illuminated the tree nicely, and Savannah smiled as she gazed at it.

"Couldn't sleep, huh?"

Savannah startled, gasping slightly at the unexpected sound of Trenner's voice.

Trying to appear as calm as possible, Savannah looked to the chair sitting to one side of the sofa. Sure enough, there sat Trenner. The darkness of the night in the room hid him well. Thus she hadn't seen him when she'd entered the room.

"No. Though I'm not sure why," Savannah fibbed. "Just the excitement of Christmas comin', I guess." Smiling at Trenner, she asked, "And you?"

She could see his jaw clench for a moment before he finally said, "I'm just near to flyin' into a rage over bein' let go by Colbalt," he confessed.

Savannah exhaled a sigh of disappointment. She'd hoped Trenner had been too wound up thinking about her the way she was wound up thinking about him—that *that* would be the reason he couldn't sleep.

"I'm sorry you're upset about it," Savannah said quietly. "But . . . I really do think you'll be happier working for Bill—for Daddy—anyway. Don't you?"

Trenner nodded. "Yep. I know I will. But it stings a feller's pride, you know? Gettin' let go that way."

He leaned forward in his chair. Savannah could see he was fiddling with something in his hands, but for the dark, she couldn't tell what it was.

"Well, I know you'll be appreciated here," Savannah said, attempting to soothe his wounded pride.

Trenner nodded. "Bill's a good man," he stated. "I really am glad to be back workin' for him. There's nobody I'd rather work for, in fact." He looked up to her, grinned, and added, "No place I'd rather be."

Savannah's insides began to warm, and she returned his smile, saying, "Well, I'm glad you agreed to stay on with us. It'll give me more time to apologize for Everett's antics today."

Instantly, Trenner's grin broadened into a smile. A low chuckle emanated from him as he said, "He's a connivin' little cuss. I'll give him that."

"Yes, he is," Savannah agreed, smiling. She loved her brother so deeply! And in her heart, she could admit to herself that his conniving and mischievous ways made him all the more adorable.

Trenner looked away from Savannah and to the tree. "It's a fine tree your family has. Fine indeed," he commented.

"Yes," Savannah sighed. "It did turn out to be especially lovely, didn't it?"

"Yep, it sure did." Trenner stood up from his

chair, and Savannah bit her lip to keep from laughing out loud as he reached around to ensure that the trap door of his long johns was secure before striding to stand just before the tree.

"In fact," he began, "there's only one little thing this tree is missin'."

Savannah's brow puckered slightly. "There is?" she asked. She was somewhat surprised, for their family had almost loaded the tree entirely with adornments. Standing, Savannah went to stand next to Trenner. "What's missin'?" she asked, studying the tree intently.

"Oh, just a little sprig of mistletoe—you know, to keep things interestin'," Trenner explained.

"Mistletoe?" Savannah asked, looking to him.

"Oh yes," Trenner said. "Mistletoe on the Christmas tree was always a tradition at our house when I was a boy."

"Mistletoe on the tree? Really?" Savannah asked. She was perplexed, for she'd never heard of mistletoe being used as an embellishment on a Christmas tree.

"Of course," Trenner assured her. "But don't worry. I come upon some mistletoe in that old hickory tree growin' out near the hitchin' post out back."

"You did?" Savannah asked. For some reason, her heart began to race. She felt her mouth flood with warm desire, found her attention had settled on Trenner's face—more specifically, his mouth.

"Yep," Trenner said, again grinning at her. Holding up one hand to show her what he held—what he'd been fiddling with while sitting in the chair next to the sofa—he said, "See? I got it right here."

"W-well, look at that," Savannah stammered in a whisper. "Mistletoe!"

"Yep," Trenner confirmed. "And I was thinkin' . . . well, that maybe we oughta give it a bit of traditional use before we hang it on the tree here. What do you think?"

Savannah found she was having difficulty drawing a breath. "A b-bit of traditional use?" she squeaked.

Trenner nodded. "Yep. I mean, truth be told, I was wishin' I'd had this earlier today—you know, when you were bathin' with me and all."

"I-I fell in. You know I only fell in," Savannah defended herself.

"Oh, I'm thinkin' it was more like you were pushed in," Trenner corrected. "But I enjoyed it all the same."

Trenner stepped toward Savannah, raised his arm, and held the mistletoe directly over her head. "So? What do you say, Miss Savannah? Are you willin' to let a banged-up ol' cowboy steal a kiss from you in front of your Christmas tree here? Hmm?"

Savannah could feel the blush of delight begin on her cheeks and travel all the way to her stockinged feet. Trenner Barnett had no need to *steal* a kiss from her. She'd willingly give it to him! Still, she knew she must hide her eagerness—her exuberance.

"Well . . . y-you have been through an awful lot these past couple of days," Savannah answered in a whisper. "I-I suppose it wouldn't be too improper to . . . to . . ."

Savannah's voice abandoned her as she watched Trenner reach over and tuck the sprig of mistletoe into the Christmas tree somewhere.

She held her breath when the handsome man reached out, taking her face between his hands and muttering, "Well, merry Christmas to me then," an instant before leaning toward her and placing a gentle kiss to her lips.

Every inch of Savannah's body tingled. She felt as if her mind were exploding with color and joy! Yet although his soft, careful kiss nearly sent her swooning, what happened next was almost her undoing. Trenner Barnett kissed her again! And again! And then, though Savannah thought there could be no more magnificent, exhilarating thing in all the world than being kissed thrice by him, her senses were sent soaring to complete rapture when his mouth began to work such a spell of coaxing hers to meet him in an impassioned kiss the likes Savannah had never known existed that she felt her knees buckle with the euphoria he was introducing to her.

Desperate to keep from slipping to the floor and away from his kiss, Savannah allowed her instincts to direct her, and they directed her to cling to him—to slip her arms up and over his shoulders, to weave her fingers up through his hair at the back of his head. Within moments, she found she was returning Trenner's kiss as fully as he was giving it, and the only coherent thought she could manage was that she never wanted their lips to part again!

One of the embers in the hearth snapped, startling Savannah, and she dropped her arms from around his neck, stepping back and thus breaking the seal of their lips.

"Oh my!" she breathlessly exclaimed. "You must think I'm—"

"I think you're wonderful, Miss Savannah," Trenner interrupted her. He reached up, caressing her cheek with the back of his hand. "And now your Christmas tree is properly ornamented . . . . and I've had the best merry Christmas I could ever have wished for."

Savannah could only stand before him, blushing vermillion.

But Trenner seemed to understand her discomfort, her concerns, for he took one of her hands in his, drew it to his lips, and kissed it. Then patting the back of her hand with reassurance, he said, "My fever broke just after supper, but I couldn't head out to the bunkhouse without takin' my last chance to kiss you, Savannah. And now I'm off in the mornin' to be a hand for your daddy."

Savannah felt tears well in her eyes. She didn't want Trenner to go to the bunkhouse! She wanted him to stay there in the parlor with her!

"Thank you for lettin' me christen that mistletoe with ya before I put it on your tree," he said. "That was surely the best Christmas present I ever did get. Ever will get, for that matter. Thank you, Savannah."

Trenner leaned down, placing a lingering kiss on Savannah's cheek. Then he strode out of the parlor and down the hall.

Savannah didn't know whether to squeal with joy or cry with despair! Never, in all her dreams, had she ever imagined a kiss could be what Trenner Barnett's kiss was—pure wonder! And now—now what? What was she supposed to do? Pretend it never happened? Admit that it did and keep it as a beloved secret for the rest of her life?

All at once, Savannah was very, very tired. Quietly she made her way back to the room she shared with her sisters and back into her bed. Even for the marvelous, wonderful, rapturous sensation that still clung to her lips—the sense of Trenner's mouth pressed to hers—even for that bliss, she knew her tired mind would finally let her rest.

• • •

Everett waited until the clock on the mantel struck eleven thirty. Then, as silently as he could, he crept from his hiding place behind the parlor sofa, making his way back to his parents' room and onto the straw mattress his father had laid there for him until Trenner was well and back in the bunkhouse.

Tucking his hands beneath his head, he stared out the window to the pale moon and silver stars scattered in the night sky. His prayers had been answered! The Lord had sent Trenner Barnett to love and care for Savannah.

"Thank you so much, Lord!" Everett whispered. "Savannah really will have a cowboy for Christmas! And all will be well."

With a smile on his face and joy in his heart, Everett closed his eyes and tried to imagine what it must be like to be Santa Claus, riding around in a sleigh all night Christmas Eve.

"Good thing he has a warm coat," Everett mumbled as he drifted off to sleep with the happiest heart any little boy ever had.

CHAPTER FIVE

Once Trenner had removed himself from the house to bunk in with the other cowboys, it seemed to Savannah that she was not the only one in the family who felt a bit less cheerful. Of course, it made perfect sense to Savannah that *she* should be less cheerful. After all, she was the one who had fallen head-over-heels in love with Trenner. The day she'd tumbled into the tub with him, and then been kissed so passionately in front of the Christmas tree that same night, had proven to her that she did, for some miraculous reason, love him!

Yet Savannah was certain that even Sadie and Amelia were a bit less excited about things—even the approach of Christmas—since Trenner had taken to the bunkhouse. As for Everett, he was always grumbling, always talking about how much fun it had been to have Trenner in the house, always asking Lottie or Bill why they'd sent Trenner out to the bunkhouse. And no amount of explaining to Everett that Trenner felt more comfortable in the bunkhouse with the other cowboys, and that it was appropriate, being that he had agreed to stay on under Bill's employ, seemed to soothe the boy.

For her part, Savannah made every effort she could to do as many out-of-doors chores as she was allowed, in an endeavor to catch even a glimpse of the man who had altogether and perhaps unwittingly stolen her heart. And on the third day since the night of their mistletoe kiss, Savannah's labors to be outside as often as possible finally gifted her with what she most wanted—to see Trenner again!

Just before noon, when her mother had mentioned needing a measure of meat from the smokehouse in preparation for supper, Savannah gleefully volunteered to fetch it for her.

"Are you sure you want to go, sweetheart?" Lottie asked. "It's quite brisk out today."

"It will serve to invigorate me," Savannah assured her mother.

Then snatching her coat from the coatrack, she inquired as to what exactly her mother needed from the smokehouse and hurried out the kitchen door.

This was to be Savannah's fourth trip outside, and with only half the day behind her. She slowed her pace, not wanting to hurry, wanting to give herself more time for circumstances to unfold—more time in having a chance at seeing Trenner.

Yet as the smokehouse was not so far from the

main house, Savannah exhaled a heavy sigh as she neared her destination.

"It's a bit cold for you to be out today, ain't it, Miss Savannah?"

Savannah gasped with the wild rush of excitement that raced through her at the sound of Trenner's voice behind her.

Spinning around as quickly as she could, she smiled—felt her cheeks pink up with delight as she saw him standing just a ways away. Savannah wondered how it could be that the man seemed even more handsome than he had only three days before. Trenner was wearing his coat and hat and a rather ragged-looking knitted scarf around his neck.

"Why, you don't even have a pair of gloves on, darlin'," Trenner said, striding toward her.

"Oh . . . well, I'm just on a quick errand for Mama . . . to the smokehouse here," Savannah said—though her hands did feel cold enough that she began rubbing them together quickly to warm them. After all, she wouldn't want Trenner to think her hands were cold and unpleasant to the touch—whether or not he would touch them.

"Let me see," Trenner said as he reached her.

Savannah bit her lip with delight at the thrill that possessed her as Trenner stripped off his own gloves, shoving them in his coat pockets before taking her hands in his.

"Why didn't your mama send your daddy or

Everett out here?" Trenner asked, frowning with concern as he rubbed Savannah's hands between his.

"I volunteered," Savannah answered.

Trenner looked surprised. "Why? It's colder'n hell out here."

Savannah giggled. "Well, that doesn't make any sense at all," she told him. She shrugged, adding, "I volunteered because . . . well, I was kind of hopin' I'd see you."

Immediately Trenner's frown of concern and inquiry changed. "Oh, you were hopin' you'd see me, were you?"

Savannah nodded. "Yep. I've already been outside three times in one mornin'," she confessed.

"Why were you hopin' to see me?" Trenner asked. His dark eyes were simmering with tomfoolery and sent a quiver traveling through Savannah's limbs. "Do you have somethin' to tell me? Were you worried that my fever mighta returned?" he offered, tugging on her hands to pull her closer.

Savannah exhaled a sigh of relief. Trenner Barnett still seemed to like her. Savannah had secretly feared that when Trenner's fever left him, so would his flirtations.

"I-I was worried about you," Savannah admitted. "I mean, I *am* worried about you."

Trenner's grin broadened into a smile, and in a

lowered, rather provocative voice, he said, "I'm flattered by your concern for my well-bein', Miss Savannah. But as you can see, I'm still as healthy as a horse."

"I *can* see that," Savannah flirted. She blushed as Trenner dropped her hands then, letting his settle at her waist as he pulled her even closer to him—nearly right up against him.

"H-how are things out in the bunkhouse?" she asked as bashfulness began to overtake her. After all, she'd been quite improperly forward in confessing to him her true reason for being out in the cold.

"Just fine," Trenner answered. "The same as any other old bunkhouse—a room full of men passin' their evenin's playin' cards and snorin'. Winter can be a bit . . . well, borin'."

Savannah nodded. "Would it help if I told you we all in the house have been a bit bored too? Especially since you left us."

Trenner chuckled. "No water sloshin' outta the tub and all in the summer kitchen, hm?"

"No indeed!" Savannah laughed.

He pulled her against him, and she could feel his breath in her hair—on her forehead when she found the courage to look up into his face.

"Hey, you wanna see somethin'?" Trenner asked, as if he'd suddenly remembered something incredible.

"Sure," Savannah agreed. "I mean, if you want

me to . . . and you're not too busy. I don't wanna keep you from your work and all."

"Naw," he assured her. "We take a break midday." Then taking one of her very warm hands in his, he led her away from the smokehouse in the direction of the privy.

"You want me to see the privy?" Savannah asked as they drew nearer to the small building.

"Nope," Trenner answered. "I want you to see the old hickory tree *near* the privy."

"Whatever for?" Savannah asked, curious.

"You'll see," he said, winking at her.

They weren't far from the old tree, and when they reached it, Trenner stopped directly beneath it, close to the trunk.

"Here it is," he unnecessarily announced.

"Yes, I see it," Savannah giggled. "But I don't understand why—"

"Just look up," Trenner interrupted.

Savannah did look up—and instantly understood. "Mistletoe!" she exclaimed. "Oh, so much of it too!"

She blushed with delight, remembering that Trenner had told her he'd retrieved the mistletoe he'd shown her the night he kissed her from the old hickory tree.

"Yep," Trenner concurred. "And you're standin' right under the biggest clump of it."

"I-I am?" Savannah asked as her heart began to race.

"Yes, ma'am, you are," Trenner mumbled as he gathered her in his arms, holding her against him. "And I have a mind to take advantage of the fact . . . again."

"You do?" Savannah asked, breathless with anticipation.

"Yes, I do," Trenner assured her.

Savannah smiled as he gazed down into her eyes.

"But first . . . I have a question."

"Yes?" Savannah's stomach knotted a bit.

Trenner wanted to kiss the girl so badly that his mouth was watering! But he didn't want her to think he was the sort of man who simply played with a woman's heart in order to satisfy his physical needs. Furthermore, no matter what Everett wished for, wanted, even prayed for, Trenner knew that Savannah would need to truly care for him. And although he already knew that he cared for Savannah, was insatiably attracted to her, owned some sort of instant feeling of protection toward her, he wanted to make sure she honestly cared for him. It might be she was just dazzled by the fact that Trenner had been the first man to ever kiss her—or at least kiss her properly.

The fact was, he'd known he had been the first man to demonstrate to Savannah how enjoyable an intimate kiss could be. He'd been able to tell by the charming inexperience she'd obviously, if not naively, revealed when their lips had first met. Yet by the time Trenner had taken her in his arms and kissed her like a man should kiss a woman—well, Savannah had molded to him, her mouth blending with his, as if they'd been made to kiss one another.

Still, Trenner harbored a secret worry that the girl was just infatuated with him because he was new to her.

And so he ventured a question. "Do you like me, Savannah?" he asked.

Savannah's lovely eyes widened in astonishment, and Trenner was nearly lost in their beautiful leaf green. Savannah's eyes put him in mind of summer—of warmth and serenity—even amid the snow and winter air surrounding them.

She blushed, glanced away from him a moment, and then confessed, "Well, I should think it would be obvious to you that I do, Mr. Barnett." She looked back to him quickly, however, the pretty pink blush draining from her cheeks even more quickly than it appeared as she asked, "Do you like me?"

Trenner reached out, brushing a stray strand of hair from her forehead. "I should think it would be obvious to you that I do, Miss Savannah."

Savannah exhaled a quiet sigh of relief, and Trenner was reassured of her affection for him.

"I just wanted to make sure you weren't

just stringin' me along for your amusement or somethin' like that," Trenner said. "I mean, you're a whole lot prettier than I could expect a girl to be who might like me and all."

Savannah arched one eyebrow suspiciously. "You're teasin' me, right?" she asked.

Trenner was perplexed. "Of course not. You're the prettiest thing I've ever seen in my whole life. And because of that, I just . . . well, I worry that you might have a whole line of beaus lined up to do your biddin' and—"

Trenner was silenced by Savannah's soft, warm palm covering his mouth.

"Now that is just ridiculous talk," she playfully scolded. "You're only sayin' that because you *know* you're the handsomest man ever born . . . and you're tryin' to make me feel better."

"Oh, I'll make you feel better, all right," Trenner mumbled as he gently pushed her hand from his mouth.

He'd been convinced enough. He could tell just by her blush, if nothing else, that she was sincere in her affection for him, and now he had to take advantage of the opportunity while he had it.

So he did. And wrapping Savannah even more tightly in his arms, he kissed her.

Oh, the rapture of Trenner Barnett's kiss! It was pure and utter bliss. Savannah melted against him, surrendering herself to him as he kissed her—as she kissed him in return. Fully as much exhilaration began coursing through her as had the night he'd kissed her in the parlor, and Savannah was simultaneously rendered breathless and intoxicated by his masculine prowess in bathing her with desire.

In fact, Savannah was disappointed when Trenner broke the seal of their kiss—though he still embraced her—gazed down at her, and said, "I want to spend time with you, Savannah—linger in your company, in conversation. But it's entirely inappropriate for one of your daddy's cowhands to—"

The sound of approaching horses startled them both then, and Savannah stepped out of Trenner's arms as he stepped back from her.

Looking in the direction from whence the sound was coming, Trenner frowned as he said, "It's your daddy . . . and the sheriff."

"Well, why on earth would the sheriff be ridin' out here with Bill?" Savannah asked.

Trenner grinned, planting a quick yet fervent kiss to her lips before saying, "Maybe I've already been found out. You know, maybe your daddy figured out I'm fixin' on romancin' you, and he's brung the sheriff out to take me to jail in town."

"Really?" Savannah gasped with horror.

But Trenner chuckled, shook his head, kissed her quickly again, and said, "Of course not, pretty baby. But I am curious. So you run on back to the house." As he turned and began to stride away, he looked back at her, adding, "And don't forget whatever it was you were fetchin' from the smokehouse, all righty?"

Savannah laughed, nodded, and hurried toward the smokehouse.

Yet as she made her way back to the house with a piece of smoked ham, a slight frown puckered her brow. What on earth was the sheriff doing coming home with Bill? she wondered.

"Well, I'll tell you one thing," Bill began. He rubbed at the whisker stubble on his chin. "I guess when ol' Colbalt lets a cowboy go, he don't want a trace of him left behind."

Sheriff Johnson nodded, adding, "I guess not."

For his part, Trenner shook his head in mild disgust. "I guess I oughta be thankful he sent my things to me though . . . instead of just tossin' them into the fire."

"Yep. I suppose it shows the man has a thread of conscience somewhere in his thick head," Sheriff Johnson offered. "I mean, it ain't much, but it is your property, Trenner."

"Yes, sir, it is," Trenner agreed. He hunkered down and rummaged through the bushel basket Walt Colbalt had had some poor cowboy ride over to deliver to Sheriff Johnson in town. In it were his extra jeans, his Sunday shirt and boots, and the small stack of cabinet cards that were the only other thing he valued, in that they were photographs of members of his family, whom he rarely heard from.

"I'm glad to have the photographs, I'll admit to that," Trenner said.

Sheriff Johnson again nodded. "I figure that's the only reason Colbalt had them sent ahead. Ain't hardly a man in the world that don't feel somethin' pluckin' his heartstrings when he sees a photograph of somebody's mama."

"That's true," Bill agreed.

Trenner straightened once more, offering a hand to Sheriff Johnson. "I thank you, Sheriff, for runnin' this stuff on out here to me."

Sheriff Johnson tipped his head to one side and drawled, "Well, I ain't out here just to play postmaster, Trenner. Truth be told, when I heard you were back, I was hopin' to get to you before Bill here had a chance to hire you on." The sheriff paused a moment and then added, "And I think you know why."

Trenner grinned. He'd suspected that Sheriff Johnson had an underlying reason for accompanying Bill and the box of Trenner's things back to Bill's ranch. After all, Bill could've easily brought the box back himself. Furthermore, Sheriff Johnson was correct. Trenner did know why the man had ridden out with Bill. At least, he had a very strong suspicion as to why.

"I may have an inklin'," Trenner admitted, grinning.

The sheriff chuckled. "I figured you might."

Bill chuckled a little as well and then said, "Yep, when I saw the sheriff in town today, first thing I thought was, 'Well, I guess it's better to have had Trenner Barnett workin' for me for three whole days than for none at all.' And I'll tell you one thing, Trenner. I can see it in your eyes since you been back—you wantin' a change in the road of your own. Ain't that right, boy?"

"Truth is, you've got plenty of hands already, Mr. Dickerson, sir," Trenner said. "You ain't in true need of me, I know that."

"Now, hang on a minute there, son," Bill began to argue, however. "I was tellin' you the truth when I said I'd rather have one of you than five other cowboys altogether. A smart cattleman, no matter how many head he has or don't have, would be a fool to let you move on without at least attemptin' to hire you. That is a fact. So don't think I hired you just because you was in a sticky spot. I hired you because I truly did want you workin' for me." Bill exhaled a heavy sigh then, smiling with understanding. "But I've seen the wear on you, boy. And I've seen the way your eyes follow my Savannah around a room too."

Trenner grinned, admiring Bill Dickerson all the more for not only his observant ways but also the fact he called Savannah his, even for the fact she was his stepdaughter and not his birth-born daughter.

"And when the sheriff asked me if I thought maybe you were finally ready to make a change," Bill continued, "I told him that I thought you probably were." He leveled an index finger at Trenner and added, "At my own expense and loss of the best cowhand I ever had, mind you."

"Thank you, sir," Trenner said to Bill.

Bill offered a hand to Trenner, and Trenner shook it.

"Now, if you ain't ready to take on what the sheriff would like for you to, then you still have a place here," Bill assured Trenner. "But if you really are as ready to make a change as I suspect you are, then there ain't no hard feelin's from me for you leavin'. All right?"

"Yes, sir," Trenner said.

Bill Dickerson was indeed a good man—a selfless, kind man with a keen business sense and an obvious gift for observation.

"I'll leave you and the sheriff to your plottin' then," Bill said. But as he turned to head into the house, he paused, looked over his shoulder, leveled the same index finger at Trenner, and in a lowered voice added, "But I'll tell you one thing. You and me are gonna have us a conversation about your intentions toward my daughter when you're done talkin' to the sheriff here, all right?"

"You bet," Trenner assured him.

"I'll be seein' you soon, Enoch," Bill said to the sheriff. "You take care now, you hear?"

"You too, Bill," the sheriff said in response.

Once Bill had disappeared into the house, Sheriff Johnson smiled at Trenner and said, "Well? It's been two years, Trenner, and I'm makin' the same offer I did before. You ready to make that change yet by chance?"

Trenner inhaled a deep breath. He tried to think rationally, but the fact was, the taste of Savannah's kiss still lingered in his mouth, and he wasn't sure he was thinking entirely straight yet. Still, he nodded in response to Sheriff Johnson's inquiry, for he *was* ready to make a change—had felt it even before the wind and snow had blown him back to Dickerson's ranch. Furthermore, although Savannah was the biggest reason he was ready, she wasn't the only reason.

"I think so," he said aloud. As a sensation of affirmation rose inside him, Trenner stated, "In fact, I don't just think it. I know it."

Sheriff Johnson exhaled the breath he'd been holding, reached out, and slapped a hand to Trenner's shoulder.

"Finally!" he said, smiling. "When can I expect you in town then?"

Trenner started to say, *Tomorrow mornin'!* but paused, thinking of Everett and his faith in prayer. After all, Trenner wanted to make sure that Savannah really did receive a cowboy for Christmas—if she'd have him, that was.

"Would it be all right with you, Sheriff, if I waited 'til the day after Christmas to move on into town . . . officially?" Trenner asked.

Sheriff Johnson nodded, removed his hat for a moment, and smoothed his thin, graying hair over his head before replacing it. "A little over a week then?" the sheriff mumbled. "I think that would be perfect, Trenner." The sheriff offered a hand to Trenner.

As Trenner accepted the man's handshake, he felt as if some unseen burden had lifted from his shoulders, and a newborn excitement about life, as well as a measure of confidence he hadn't even known he was missing, welled up inside him, filling his heart and mind with fresh ambition. He owned a sudden awareness that his life was beginning again, and as he stood talking with Sheriff Johnson, Trenner Barnett felt better than he had in a very long time.

"What do you suppose they're talkin' about?" Sadie asked as she peered up over the windowsill and out to where Trenner and Sheriff Johnson stood in seemingly friendly conversation.

"How on earth would I know?" Savannah asked. In truth, she was irritated that she didn't know. Her curiosity was piqued even more that Sadie's and Amelia's was—she knew it was.

"Maybe Trenner has become an outlaw!" Amelia gasped in a whisper. "Maybe Sheriff Johnson has come to take him to jail . . . or string him up in a tree!"

"Oh, don't be insipid, Amelia," Sadie scolded. "If Trenner was an outlaw, the sheriff would've simply shot him on sight. Or Daddy would've, for that matter."

"He ain't an outlaw," Everett said, following the gazes of his three sisters as he peered out through the parlor window too. "He's the finest cowboy Daddy has ever known. Daddy says Sheriff Johnson just brung some of Trenner's things out to him that that nasty old Mr. Colbalt sent on."

"Well, if you know so much," Sadie began, "what *are* Trenner and Sheriff Johnson talkin' about?"

When Everett didn't answer, Savannah, Sadie, and Amelia all three turned their heads from peering out the parlor window to Everett.

"Well?" Amelia urged.

But Everett shrugged. "How should I know?" Everett exclaimed in a conspiratorial whisper. "Maybe Daddy saw Trenner kissin' on Savannah out by the privy as they rode up, and Sheriff Johnson's makin' sure Trenner ain't some sort of rounder or somethin'."

"What?" Sadie and Amelia exclaimed.

Savannah wondered how their necks hadn't

snapped—for the force and speed with which they turned their heads to look at her seemed as if it could've done exactly that.

"He kissed you?" Sadie squealed with excitement. "And you didn't tell Amelia and me?"

"Well, I . . . I . . ." Savannah stammered.

"It weren't the first time neither," Everett offered with a smile.

"How do you know?" Savannah asked, mortified that her little brother knew so much about it.

"I . . . I, um . . . I'm just guessin'," Everett said. "I mean, from the way he was kissin' you out under the old hickory a while ago, I was just guessin' it weren't the first time, Savannah."

Sadie nearly leapt to her feet, pulled Amelia to hers, smiled at Savannah, and said, "Come on to our room, girls. It's obvious we need to have talk."

"Can I come along?" Everett asked.

"No indeed!" Sadie giggled. "It sounds to me like you know too much already."

Everett's happy expression faded. So kissing him on one cheek, Savannah said, "And besides, we need you to keep watchin' so we can find out what Sheriff Johnson wants with Trenner, all right?"

"You are rather good at gleanin' information after all, Everett, honey," Amelia added.

"Undoubtedly," Sadie added, tousling the boy's

straw hair and kissing him sweetly on the cheek.

Immediately, Everett brightened, the smile of mischief that Savannah so adored returning to his face.

"That's true!" he exclaimed in a whisper. "Somethin' is definitely goin' on, and I mean to find out what it is!"

"You do that, sweet pea," Amelia said. She kissed his cheek as well, adding, "But don't forget to tell us, okeydokey?"

"I sure won't, Amelia," Everett promised.

"Now you come on back here, Savannah, and tell us all about it," Sadie said as she linked her arm with Savannah's.

"Yes, do," Amelia confirmed, linking her arm with Savannah's free one. "I cannot believe you kept this from us, Savannah! After all, it was Sadie and me that suggested you marry Trenner in the first place."

"No, it wasn't!" Everett announced, leaping to his feet. The expression on his face was of pure offense at being slighted somehow.

"What do you mean, Everett?" Savannah asked.

But her little brother seemed to reconsider his outburst. "Oh . . . oh, nothin' really," Everett stammered. "I just . . . I just . . . well, I best get back to tryin' to figure out what the sheriff wants with Trenner. You girls have fun with your hen-peckin'."

And like a flash of lightning, Everett had raced

from the parlor, through the kitchen, and out the back door.

"So?" Amelia asked as she and Sadie practically dragged Savannah to their bedroom. "Has Trenner asked to escort you to the town social next week?"

"Has he asked Daddy if he can court you yet?" Sadie inquired.

"No! No, not at all!" Savannah exclaimed. "I-I don't even know what his feelin's are exactly where I'm concerned."

"Well, you just tell us everythin' that has gone on, and we'll tell you what he's feelin'," Sadie giggled as the three young ladies entered their bedroom, closing the door and bolting it behind them.

Lottie exhaled a sigh of satisfaction. Oh, she didn't let on at all—especially not to Savannah—but she was Savannah's mother and therefore had instantly recognized that Trenner Barnett was quickly claiming her daughter's heart for his own. Lottie had also overheard Everett praying for his sister on several occasions—praying that the Lord would send Savannah a cowboy for Christmas. And though she knew her young, faithful son hadn't been so surprised the night the storm had blown Trenner through the Dickersons' front door, Lottie had been.

Oh, she'd scolded herself on many occasions

since for not having the faith Everett did. Fact was, Lottie had even apologized to God and His Son in her prayers for not having the faith of a child where Trenner's appearance was concerned. Still, she'd vowed to do better—to do everything in her power to make sure the young man lived, thrived, and was not taken ill with pneumonia so that the miracle Everett had prayed for could be fulfilled.

"The faith of a child," Lottie sighed as she began to knead the bread dough that had been rising all morning. "Dear Lord . . . thank you for the faith of children to show us grown-ups the way."

"Amen," Bill said from his seat at the table.

Lottie turned and smiled lovingly at her husband—silently giving thanks to the same Heavenly Father and Savior of the world, who'd blessed her with her own miracle in bringing Bill to love her and her children, and to love in return.

CHAPTER SIX

"Warm enough?" Trenner asked.

"Yes," Savannah answered—though, in truth, she knew she'd be much warmer were she wrapped tightly in Trenner's strong embrace. Even though the quilts and furs kept the chill of the brisk winter's night at bay, Trenner's arms provided a thoroughgoing warmth that could not be rivaled.

Savannah sighed as Trenner switched the lines to one hand so that his other could be free to hold Savannah's under the quilts and furs covering their laps. As the sleigh cut through the snow toward town, Savannah marveled at the beauty of the night.

It was December 23—nearly Christmas—and the clear night sky seemed swathed in black velvet embellished with diamonds of every size that captured moonlight and seemed to blow kisses of it as they twinkled. A light frost had begun to fall—not snow but frost. This also lent a sense of magic to the evening, for it sparkled as Savannah imagined diamond dust would, were it to be sifted down from the heavens to land on the warm noses and fluttering eyelashes of every child on the way to the town social that night.

"It's such a beautiful night!" Savannah exclaimed in a breathy, awestruck sigh. "It makes me almost wish that we could just sleigh ride for hours together out in it . . . not even go to the social."

"*Almost* wish?" Trenner asked, feigning offense. "For my part of it, I'd rather take you sleigh ridin' all night long and all by myself . . . and I don't *almost* wish it. I *do* wish it."

Savannah giggled, linking her arm with his. "We're just lucky Daddy let us take the extra sleigh on our own. At least we can have our own conversation."

Trenner looked back over his shoulder to where the rest of the Dickerson family rode with a team of horses pulling the much larger sleigh than the one-horse open sleigh he and Savannah were riding in.

"Oh, I'm glad of that too," Trenner admitted. "And you're right. At least we have our own conversation." He chuckled, adding, "At least I can tell you that I'd like nothin' more than to spend the entire night kissin' on you up in the hayloft, and no one can hear me say it."

Savannah again giggled, delighted with his flirting.

"At least I can say that your pretty eyes make me feel like my stomach's gonna leap right out of my throat when I look at you and that I sure am glad them rustlers out-rid me that night and that I was taken with fever enough to ask your daddy for shelter . . . and that the day you tumbled into the bathtub with me, I figured I'd died and gone to heaven for a minute. And no one, especially Everett, can hear me sayin' it to you."

Savannah laughed. "I'm still mortified that I ended up in your tub!" Savannah admitted. "Why, I think women have gone to jail for less!"

Trenner laughed. "Oh, I highly doubt that, darlin'," he assured her.

Savannah sighed once more, this time with utter contentment. Trenner Barnett loved her—and she loved him! They'd confessed their love to one another only one week after having met. Of course, other than Sadie and Amelia—and most likely Everett—no one else in all the world knew they were in love. Oh, certainly Savannah's mother and stepfather knew they liked each other. After all, Trenner had gone to Bill the night before, asking permission to officially court Savannah and also if they could ride alone together to the town social. But Savannah doubted that either her mother or Bill knew the true depth of their feelings for one another. In fact, Savannah was quite proud of how secretive she and Trenner had managed to be, meeting whenever and wherever they could to talk, share stories of their lives and their families, and of course share warm embraces and impassioned kisses. Savannah could even feel pride rising in her bosom as the sleigh drew them ever nearer to town and the town Christmas social. Once she walked in on the arm of Trenner Barnett, everyone would know that, through some heaven-sent miracle, Savannah Ambrose had managed to capture the attention of the most wonderful man ever born!

Naturally, Savannah knew she shouldn't feel prideful about owning Trenner's affections. It was quite nearly sinful. But she felt it all the same. And it wasn't just Trenner's good looks, uniquely good character, and the fact that she would be the envy of every young woman in town that caused her pride to swell. It was because, in being able to capture the attention of Trenner Barnett—the most handsome, strong, kind, heroic, and archetypal man she'd ever known—she had begun to believe she truly was of worth as a person, as a woman. If Trenner Barnett with his impeccable integrity and breathtaking allure could find interest and value in Savannah, then so should Savannah.

It was a truth that Trenner had brought the best of Savannah to the surface. Furthermore, he'd healed her wounded heart—a heart wounded by loss, insecurity, and worry. In Trenner's presence, Savannah found she never felt fearful—or at least that she felt courageous and able to climb whatever mountain of tribulation that might be placed before her. In Trenner's arms, Savannah also felt love and desire to degrees she'd never before known even existed. Trenner had taken over her heart—taken up residence inside her with her soul.

True, he hadn't yet proposed marriage to her. But Savannah figured that few men did propose after knowing a woman only a bit more than one week. Still, she sensed that he would—one day he would.

From the course of their conversations—and there had been many since their meeting—Savannah had gleaned that Trenner felt a cowboy had nothing to offer a woman, that a cowboy was a lonely occupation that kept men away from family and friends and did not pay enough in wages to keep a wife and children. No amount of argument from Savannah would sway him to think differently either. Yet Trenner had confessed to her that he was thinking of changing occupations but that he had more things to work out in his mind before he could divulge the details to her. And whenever Savannah impatiently, yet playfully, pressed him to share his plans, Trenner would simply chuckle, tell her she would spoil Christmas for herself if she kept trying to get him to reveal his musings too soon, and end their conversation with a deep, warm, moist kiss of such blazing passion, Savannah would be eager to let him keep his secrets so that she could continue enjoying the perfect flavor of his kiss.

And so Savannah was not impatient to know what Trenner had planned as far as his change in occupation or when he planned to change it. She trusted him—wholeheartedly trusted him. She would wait until Christmas, and then she would press him once more. And if by the end of Christmas Day he still refused to reveal his intentions toward her, Savannah had settled herself on being content to be in his arms—her questions silenced by his mouth claiming hers.

The town hall was in sight now, bright and brilliant in the night with lamps and candles inside making it appear as if the sun itself had set inside. Sleigh bells were ringing all along the main street as people arrived for the social.

"Looks bright and cheery enough," Trenner said as he pulled the horse to a halt before the general store. Winking at Savannah, he asked, "Wonder if there'll be any mistletoe hangin' in there. I'd be mighty happy to catch you under it and give everyone in town somethin' to gossip about through the hailin' in of the New Year."

"I'd be mighty happy to oblige you in doin' just that," Savannah said, smiling at him.

Trenner smiled at her, and Savannah felt her breath catch in her throat—for his dark eyes fairly simmered with emotion as he gazed at her.

"It ain't too late, you know," he said.

"For what?" Savannah giggled.

"Well, your daddy is tyin' his team up across the way, and I ain't tied up yet," he began explaining. "One slap of the lines to the back of ol' Penny here, and we're off to go sleigh ridin' all night on our own."

"Are you tryin' to tempt me into rebellion, scandal, and a soiled reputation, Mr. Barnett?" Savannah asked. Oh, how she wanted to kiss him—to be in his arms and never again have to leave them.

"Me?" Trenner quietly exclaimed. "You're the one temptin' me into rebellion, scandal, and a soiled reputation, sittin' there lookin' so beautiful in your new red dress. You make me wanna just carry you on up to some hayloft and have my way with you." He winked at her. "And you accusin' me of bein' the tempter."

"I've always loved red," Savannah said. "And this is the first time in all my life my mama allowed me to make a red dress. And I'll have you know, I made it this week, in hopes that *you* would notice me."

Trenner smiled, and again his eyes simmered with restrained passion as he looked at her. "Oh, I noticed you all right. I noticed you the first time I ever laid eyes on you . . . and I ain't quit noticin' you since."

"My, my, my!" Savannah said as Trenner stepped out of the sleigh and began to secure

Penny to a post. "Aren't you just the imp of a flirt tonight."

"Oh, darlin', if you only knew the things I *think* of sayin' but don't," Trenner said, offering a hand to help Savannah step out of the sleigh.

"Someday will you say everything you think of sayin' to me too? And not just the things you do say?" Savannah asked as she stood in the snow gazing up at him.

"I certainly will," Trenner promised. "I most certainly will."

"Oh, I'm so excited I think I'm just gonna burst!" Amelia said, hurrying over to Savannah and linking arms with her.

Sadie joined them as well, smiling as she said, "Our poor little brother. He's just terrified that some girl is gonna catch him under the mistletoe and kiss him square on the lips! I swear he talked about nothin' else all the way to town!"

"That's 'cause he's hopin' it will happen," Trenner explained. "It'll probably ruin his Christmas if some little filly don't do it."

Savannah, Sadie, and Amelia all looked to Trenner, simultaneously asking, "Really?"

"Oh, absolutely," Trenner assured them. "There ain't a boy in all the world who don't wanna kiss from a girl more than anything at Everett's age. Don't let him fool you. He ain't afraid it's gonna happen. He's worried it won't."

Savannah laughed with her sisters and her lover.

Life was so delicious! And as they all walked together, along with Everett, Bill, and Lottie, Savannah's heart swelled with not only the joy of the season and the understanding of what it stood for but also for the fact that her family was whole and that, one day, she and Trenner would expand it even further.

"Isn't everything just lovely?" Sadie asked as she approached Savannah and Trenner. She was on the arm of Clay Picket and looked as radiant as a new bride. "I mean, can you believe how perfectly festive everything is?"

"Clay," Trenner greeted, offering a hand to the tall young man escorting Sadie.

"Trenner," Clay responded, shaking Trenner's hand. "I bet ol' Bill Dickerson is glad you came back around, isn't he?" Clay asked.

Savannah couldn't help but notice the contrast between Trenner and Clay. Oh, Clay Picket was a handsome man in his own right—tall, well-built, and strong, with dusty blond hair and blue eyes. But he seemed rather plain when standing before Trenner Barnett. Again Savannah felt an impish amount of pride welling in her and silently scolded herself for it.

Trenner shrugged. "I sure hope so," Trenner responded. "He's the best I've ever worked for, so I hope I can measure up."

"Oh, I remember him singin' your praises

constantly when you were cowboyin' for him before," Clay laughed. "I doubt he's got anything less to say about ya now."

The music began again, and Savannah giggled a little when Sadie cleared her throat in offering a hint to Clay that she'd like to be asked to dance.

Clay, gentleman that he was, and sweet on Sadie as he was, immediately smiled at Sadie and asked, "May I have this dance, Miss Sadie?"

"Why, of course, Picket!' Sadie answered with excitement. "Thank you for askin' again."

Savannah heard Trenner chuckle as she and he watched Clay lead Sadie to the dance floor.

Savannah cleared her throat the way Sadie had done, and Trenner, feigning that he was startled by the little noise, looked to her and asked, "May I have this dance, Miss Savannah?"

Savannah fanned her face with one hand, feigning a blush and answered, "Why, of course, Mr. Barnett! I'd be delighted!"

Of course, Trenner had asked Savannah to dance many, many times throughout the night. And each time had been simply a dream come true for Savannah. Still, as Trenner took her in his arms, she found that she was no less giddy than she had been every other time they'd danced.

"It's a lovely social, isn't it?" Savannah asked him as they waltzed.

"It certainly is," Trenner agreed, "though I do

admit that your mama's pumpkin pie is by far the best I've tasted here tonight."

Savannah nodded. "Mama is the best cook! But I did enjoy Mrs. Johnson's stuffin', didn't you?"

Trenner nodded. "I sure did."

Savannah sighed as she listened to the men playing their fiddles so that everyone could dance—a lovely version of the Tennessee waltz. Everything in the room was so bright and pretty! Mrs. Johnson had even lent her fine collection of German glass ornaments as adornments for the enormous Christmas tree that stood in one corner. The smells of warm supper rolls—slathered in butter—pumpkin, apple, and mincemeat pies, and mulled cider filled the air. Children played chase, running around the room but staying close to the walls so as not to infringe on the adults' fun. Little girls wore every color of ribbon in their hair, and little boys wore their best knickers and bow ties. Ladies had woven flowers through their coiffures, and the hat racks placed hither and yon by every entrance to the hall were simply straining to hold all the gentlemen's hats.

"And here we go," Trenner said, drawing Savannah's attention to Sheriff Johnson.

Savannah laughed when she saw Sheriff Johnson hand his youngest daughter, Sally, a sprig of mistletoe. At first, the girl looked bashful. But much to Savannah's surprise and delight, Sally Johnson took off like a bunny rabbit toward

Everett, sneaked up behind him, and, holding the mistletoe over her head, tapped him on the shoulder.

Everett turned around to see Sally holding the mistletoe over her head, and Savannah held her breath.

"Oh, surely he won't reject her, will he, Trenner?" Savannah asked in an anxious whisper.

"Trust me, sweetheart," Trenner said. "He ain't gonna say no. Just you watch."

Savannah exhaled a sigh of relief and giggled as she watched Everett roll his eyes in feigning agitation a moment before he leaned forward and met Sally Johnson's pucker to exchange a Christmas kiss with her.

"Oh, how cute!" Savannah quietly exclaimed. "Did you see that, Trenner? Did you see how adorable that was?"

Trenner chuckled. "I sure did. The boy got his Christmas kiss. Now we can relax and really enjoy the rest of the night, hmm?"

Savannah nodded as Trenner resumed waltzing with her. Savannah hadn't even noticed that they'd paused in their dance to watch Everett and Sally—for elation was all she knew when she was in Trenner's arms.

"Sheriff! Sheriff Johnson!"

The music stopped, and everyone looked to the door to see what the commotion was.

"It's Lucas Smith," Trenner mumbled as he

abruptly stopped their waltz. "Somethin' must be wrong."

Lucas Smith was a cowboy working the winter for Savannah's daddy, Bill. And it didn't take long for everyone in the room to see that the man was bleeding from his left arm and looked as if he'd ridden to hell and back.

"What's wrong, Lucas?" Savannah heard Bill ask as most of the men in the room gathered around the fatigued and injured cowboy.

"Rustlers," Lucas breathed. "Th-they cut out about five or six head, Mr. Dickerson. Me and Angus rode out after 'em, but they started shootin', and we figured one of us better just ride for help. And since I was hit . . . well, Angus is still trackin' 'em."

"Oh no!" Savannah gasped. A fearful nausea began to knead her stomach.

"Probably the same ones that hit Colbalt's place a couple of weeks back," Savannah heard Sheriff Johnson say. "Which way did they head out, boy?"

"N-north," Lucas said.

"Let me through," Doctor Haralson said, making his way through the crowd. He looked at Lucas's arm and then turned and said, "Let's get the boy back to my office."

Savannah looked up to see Trenner staring down at her. He wore a deep frown on his brow.

"I was waitin' 'til Christmas to tell you,

Savannah," he said. Something in the firm sound of his voice caused Savannah's already upset stomach to churn even worse with anxiety.

"To tell me what?" she asked.

"I-I hate to ask you, Trenner," Sheriff Johnson asked as he strode directly toward Trenner. "I know you wanted to wait, but these are probably the same rustlers that shot you up over Colbalt's cattle . . . and I could sure use you tonight."

Savannah watched, stunned as Sheriff Johnson reached into his coat pocket, retrieved something, and held it out toward Trenner.

"Deputy," Savannah read aloud. As panic washed over her, she clung to Trenner's arm, asking, "Is this what you wouldn't tell me? You're . . . you're a . . . a . . ."

"Lawman," Trenner finished for her. Inhaling a deep breath, Trenner did not pause a moment in snatching the bronze star badge from Sheriff Johnson's hand and pinning it to his coat.

Then, taking a still stunned Savannah by the shoulders, he stared directly into her eyes, saying, "This is a good thing, Savannah. It'll allow us to . . . I need to explain . . . there's too much to tell you right now."

"A-all right," Savannah stammered. "Just . . . just go." Then grabbing hold of his coat lapels and fisting them tightly in her hands, she said, "But you better come back . . . because you have a lot of explainin' to do!"

"I know," Trenner said.

And then, right there in front of everybody in town, Trenner gathered Savannah into his arms and kissed her—claimed her mouth in a powerful, driven promise that he would return.

Savannah heard several women gasp, no doubt horrified by the public display of intimacy. But she didn't care what anyone thought and kissed Trenner full as passionately as he kissed her.

Breaking the seal of their kiss, Trenner told her, "I'll be back as quick as I can. Wait for me. Promise."

"Of course," Savannah promised as tears filled her eyes.

Trenner forced a slight grin, adding, "Wait for me by the Christmas tree in your mama's parlor, darlin'. I'll come there first thing when we're back."

"I will," Savannah breathed.

"I need more men to ride out with us!" Sheriff Johnson hollered into the crowd. "We gotta stop these rustlers before they succeed in killin' one of our boys!"

"Well, I'll tell you one thing," Bill said, stepping up to stand with the sheriff and Trenner. "I ain't sittin' home on my haunches this time. No sirree!"

Savannah felt her mother's arm link with her own—knew that her mother was just as frightened for Bill's safety as Savannah was for

Trenner's—and she began to feel a harsh dizziness overtake her.

Willing herself to be strong—insisting to her dizzy mind that she would not swoon and thereby show weakness to Trenner, Bill, or anyone else—Savannah clenched her jaw tightly, forcing herself to watch as Sheriff Johnson, his new deputy, Trenner Barnett, and several other men left the town hall. She knew that no doubt the sleigh that had so romantically conveyed her and Trenner to the Christmas social would now serve to take Trenner and her father home to tack up their own mounts—and that they would then set out in search of the rustlers.

"I-I don't want to spoil anyone's evenin'," Lottie said as Sadie and Amelia joined her and Savannah in clinging together for support. "But I rather think we should head home . . . b-before it grows too late."

"Yes, Mama," Amelia agreed aloud. For her part, Sadie merely nodded as she stood staring out the door after her father and the others in utter disbelief—for Clay Picket had joined Sheriff Johnson's posse as well.

"But . . . but Trenner can't be a lawman!" Everett exclaimed, bursting into tears. "I-I asked God for a cowboy for Savannah, and he sent Trenner. But if he's a lawman . . . and he ain't a cowboy no more . . . then what does that mean?"

Suddenly snapping from her state of shock in

that Trenner was now a deputy lawman and off to chase a dangerous gang of rustlers, Savannah dropped to her knees in front of her little brother.

Taking Everett's shoulders, she directed him to look at her and through her own tears asked, "What do you mean, Everett? What do you mean you asked God to send a cowboy for me for Christmas?"

Everett sniffled, angrily wiping the tears from his cheeks. "I-I've been prayin' for weeks now, Savannah," he sobbed. "I've been prayin' to God and Jesus . . . that they'd send you a cowboy to love you . . . to marry you . . . and that they'd send him for Christmas! And then Trenner showed up, and I knew they'd been listenin' to me! And when I told Trenner—"

"You *told* Trenner?" Savannah asked, horrified with humiliation. "You told Trenner that you asked for a cowboy to come and marry me? When?"

"The very night he came, after Mama sent him to bed," Everett cried. "I told him that he had to get better . . . 'cause he was meant to marry you. But now . . . now he's gone off and joined the law, and he ain't a cowboy no more and . . . oh, Mama!" Everett cried, throwing himself against his mother. "Everything is all ruined forever now!"

Slowly, Savannah stood up from her knees. Glancing around, she wondered how many people had heard her little brother confess to coercing Trenner Barnett into becoming romantically involved with her.

"I see what you're thinkin', Savannah Rose," Lottie said, her voice firm even for the tears streaming down her cheeks. "And don't you go thinkin' it any longer, do you hear me? That boy has loved you from the minute he set eyes on you. And whether it was God or chance, he loves you truly . . . and don't you spend one moment thinkin' different. Do you hear me?"

Savannah remained perfectly still, however, as she tried to sort everything out in her mind.

"I asked, do you hear me, Savannah Rose?" Lottie repeated.

At last Savannah looked to where her mother stood—Everett clinging to her waist, Sadie and Amelia hanging on her shoulders. Lottie Dickerson looked exactly like a statue of strength—as if she were there supporting everyone else without anyone to support her.

Gulping with dread, fear, heartache, doubt, and desperation, Savannah vowed, as ever she had from the moment her father had died years before, that she would not be another burden for her mother to bear.

Therefore, she answered, "Yes, Mama."

"Let's just go home, Mama. Please?" Everett quietly asked. "I need to do some talkin' with the Lord."

• • •

Lottie looked down at her young son, still so full of faith and hope.

"Of course, darlin'," she said. "Let's get home and get the house all cozy and warm for your daddy and Trenner to come home to, shall we? Tomorrow's Christmas Eve, and we've still got gifts to prepare, don't we?"

Everett sighed with relief and comfort. "Yes, we do," he said.

Lottie looked to Savannah, her heart breaking a little as she recognized two things in her daughter's eyes: doubt and resolve. The doubt, Lottie knew, was from wondering whether Trenner Barnett truly loved her or was just trying to fulfill Everett's dire wish. The presence of powerful resolve she saw in Savannah's eyes was all too painfully familiar—resolve to be strong, selfless, and happy for Lottie's sake.

"Come on, Mama," Sadie said then. "Let's get home like you said." Bending down to kiss Everett's cheek, Lottie watched as Sadie then took Everett's hand in hers. "I need some help with somethin' I'm workin' on for Daddy for Christmas, Everett. Do you think that when we get home, if I read you a storybook or two first, you'd be willin' to help me?"

Everett brushed more tears from his eyes. "I need a few minutes with the Lord first, Sadie.

Then I sure would be glad to help you . . . and to hear stories."

"Good," Sadie said. "Then let's get on home."

As the Dickerson family started to leave the town hall, Savannah turned and looked back at the grand room that had been so bright, cheerful, and full of joy only minutes before. Afraid that perhaps everyone in town had already taken to gossiping about the fact that Savannah Ambrose was so desperate for a man that her little brother had had to pray for one to come to her, she was somewhat relieved when she saw that, instead, everyone was busy cleaning up the hall. The party had ended the moment it was reported that Bill Dickerson's cowhand had been injured and that cattle had been stolen. Savannah was relieved that the gossip had not begun—at least not yet.

"Everyone in this hall knows, without a doubt, that that handsome young deputy of yours is yours for the takin', Savannah," Mrs. Johnson said.

Savannah looked to her and tried to smile.

Mrs. Johnson took one of Savannah's hands in her own, squeezing it with reassurance as she said, "Enoch confided in me that Trenner Barnett is plannin' his entire future centered on you, Savannah. Don't doubt the man simply because God may have had a hand in gettin' the two of you together. That man loves you, girl! That kiss he done planted on you before he left?" Mrs. Johnson actually blushed as she lowered her voice and said, "Well, Enoch ain't never kissed me the likes of that any place other than the privacy of our own bedroom! Trenner Barnett loves you, so don't you spend one more moment doubtin' it, all right?"

Savannah did feel a measure of her fear and doubt begin to flitter away. "I'll try not to."

But Mrs. Johnson shook her head. "No. You won't."

The woman smiled as Sally ran up and tugged on her arm.

"Will Everett's daddy be all right, Mama?" Sally asked. "Everett looked so sad just now."

Mrs. Johnson nodded. "Yes, darlin'. Mr. Dickerson will be fine. And so will Daddy and Mr. Barnett and all the others. Don't you worry."

"Okay, Mama. I won't," Sally said.

"And don't *you* worry either, Savannah," Mrs. Johnson reiterated. "That kiss Trenner Barnett gave you before he left with Enoch . . . it's proof enough for everyone else that witnessed it. So have faith in your man."

Savannah nodded. "I will."

"Good." Mrs. Johnson approved, smiling. "Now you all get home and get ready for Christmas Eve tomorrow. No doubt our menfolk will be plum tuckered out when they get back."

"Yes, ma'am," Savannah assured her.

Then, as she hurried out to the sleigh to join her sisters, brother, and mother, Savannah looked up just in time to see the North Star shining brilliantly overhead. It was a beautiful sight, and her thoughts settled in her mind. *So what if Everett prayed for Trenner and God answered my brother's loving, thoughtful prayer for me? The Lord and God are loving, so why wouldn't they bring together two people who were perfect for one another? Two people who would love each other like few people did?*

Climbing into the sleigh, Savannah wrapped her arms around Everett. "Thank you, Everett!" she whispered into his ear. "Thank you for prayin' for Trenner to come to me."

Everett smiled, though tentatively. "So you ain't mad at me anymore, Savannah?"

Savannah shook her head. "I was never mad at you, sweet pea. Only worried that Trenner didn't really care for me . . . that he just wanted to make your wish come true."

Everett arched his brows with skepticism. "Do you really think I woulda worked it out so that you ended up in the bathtub with him if I didn't know for sure he was gonna fall in love with you, Savannah?"

"What?" Lottie exclaimed sharply, causing the team of horses to surge forward.

Even for all the worry and anxiety each member

of the family felt over the well-being and safety of their father and Trenner, Sadie, Amelia, and Savannah all burst into laughter at the startled expression on their mother's face as she struggled to regain control of the team pulling the sleigh.

"What are you talkin' about, Everett?" Lottie asked. "What's all this about Savannah bein' in a tub with Trenner?"

"Not now, Mama," Everett said as he folded his hands and bowed his head. Winking at Savannah, he grinned, adding, "I think we should pray for Daddy and Trenner and all the other men, right this very minute."

"Me too," Amelia agreed, bowing her head.

"But—" Lottie began.

"Dear Lord, please watch over Daddy and Trenner . . . oh, and Clay Picket too, bein' that Sadie's sweet on him. Actually, Lord, please watch over all the men in the posse goin' after the rustlers."

Savannah and Sadie exchanged glances of amused understanding. Certainly offering a prayer for the posse's safety was something that must be done as quickly as possible. But Savannah, Sadie, Amelia, and most likely their mother all understood that Everett was also trying to divert his mother's attention away from inquiring further about the bathtub incident with Trenner and Savannah.

"Amen," Lottie said.

"And, Lord—" Everett continued, however.

"Do you think he'll pray all the way home?" Sadie asked Savannah in a whisper.

"He's liable to try," Savannah answered, smiling.

"Please help Mama to be patient with me and know that I'm just tryin' to help things along where my sisters are concerned," Everett continued to pray.

Savannah, Sadie, and Amelia each allowed a quiet giggle to escape them as they heard Lottie sigh in resigning herself to the fact that if she pressed the bathtub issue, her son would never give her an amen and end his praying.

"Oh, the faith of a child," Lottie said aloud as a smile spread across her face.

CHAPTER SEVEN

Christmas Eve dawned cloudy and cold. As Savannah and her siblings sat at the breakfast table enjoying warm bread and berry jam, Savannah couldn't help but think of Trenner and Bill still riding in such miserable weather. At least it wasn't snowing—not where the ranch and house sat anyway.

Everyone from Lottie down to Everett had passed a restless, miserable night fraught with worry and anxiety. And when each member of the family woke to find that the posse that had set out after the rustlers the night before had obviously not returned yet, the worry and anxiety increased tenfold.

"Do you think Daddy and Trenner are all right, Mama?" Everett asked for the umpteenth time.

Savannah admired her mother's patience as she smiled and calmly answered, yet again, "Yes, sweet pea. I'm sure they're fine."

Still, every sound—every snapping twig from a snow- and frost-laden tree, every whinny from a horse out in the barn, any sound at all—found the entire family freezing still where they sat and listening to see whether said sound was the posse returning.

When breakfast had stretched far too long because of worry, Lottie finally stood up and said, “Let’s each get busy with somethin’. Bakin’, dustin’, preparin’ gifts—I don’t care what. I just know that sittin’ here stewin’ isn’t helpin’ us one bit.”

“All right, Mama,” Everett agreed first. He looked to Amelia, asking, “Wanna play checkers with me, Amelia?”

“You bet,” Amelia said, forcing a smile.

Savannah knew Amelia felt less like playing checkers than anyone and admired her all the more for being willing to entertain Everett for a while.

Rising from her chair and going to the window, Savannah pulled her shawl more tightly around her shoulders. “It looks so cold out today,” she remarked. “I can’t imagine how cold it was last night.”

“Daddy will be fine,” Sadie offered. “Trenner too. They’re both as tough as cowhide and know how to keep safe and warm in bad weather.”

Savannah turned, offering a smile of thanks to her older sister. “I know,” she said. “I just wish they’d come home is all.”

“Did you finish knittin’ that scarf you were workin’ on, Savannah?” Lottie asked. “Because if you’re plannin’ on givin’ it to Trenner for

Christmas . . . well, he sure is in need of it."

Savannah smiled. "Yes, I am . . . and don't I know it!"

"Mama, you remember Johnny Bradshaw?" Everett asked.

"Of course," Lottie answered. "You and him used to play for hours on end when you were little."

Everett nodded. "Well, I'm glad you're makin' Trenner a new scarf, Savannah, because that scarf Trenner was wearin' the night he blew in . . . well, it reminds me exactly of that nasty old blue snot-rag Johnny Bradshaw used to carry around with him everywhere." Everett gagged a little at the memory of Johnny Bradshaw's snot-rag.

"Oh my!" Lottie exclaimed. "I just couldn't abide that rag of Johnny's any longer. That's why it disappeared one day when he was over to play with you, Everett."

Savannah giggled. "Yep. It disappeared right into the fire of the cookstove, thanks to Mama."

Everett laughed, slapping his leg with wild amusement. "Is that what happened to that nasty ol' thing, Mama?" he asked through his laughter.

"Indeed it is, darlin'," Lottie admitted as she began to laugh as well.

Even though Sadie and Amelia had never been witness to the grimy gore of Johnny Bradshaw's snot-rag, they were laughing as well—overcome with mirth and just the mere imagery of it, as well as the merriment the memory had washed over Lottie, Savannah, and Everett.

"Remember how he used to twist up one corner of that rag and then shove it up his nose, wring it around a few times, and then pull it out and look at it?" Everett asked, tears of joviality running from the corners of his eyes.

"I know! I know!" Lottie laughed. "I always wondered . . . what did he expect to find in there? Gold nuggets or somethin'?"

Everyone melted into robust, nearly painful chortles then.

"How nauseating!" Sadie managed to exclaim.

"Oh, you have no idea!" Lottie laughed.

"Mama? You took Johnny's snot-rag and threw it in the fire?" Everett asked, trying to catch his breath.

"I did," Lottie admitted, dabbing at the tears of mirth in her eyes with the hem of her apron.

"Oh, thank you, Mama!" Everett sighed, going to where his mother stood and throwing his arms around her waist. "I used to think I couldn't stand to play with Johnny no more, even though I liked his company, because that old snot-rag about sent me to throwin' up every time he pulled it out of his pocket."

"Well, isn't that what every handkerchief is?" Amelia asked. "Somethin' a man uses to take what's *in* his nose *out* . . . and put it in his pocket?"

Again the family erupted into laughter that could be heard all the way up to heaven.

And even though she was laughing so hard tears were running from the corners of her eyes, Savannah felt another kind of joy welling in her as well—not amusement but great happiness in realizing that they were indeed a family! Bill, Sadie, Amelia—they were family now, not just a stepfather and stepsisters. They'd truly grown to be a family, and it had been solidified over the past couple of weeks. It was a wonderful and benevolent gift given to them by the Son of God himself—a gift given to them during the season that celebrated His own birth.

"What in tarnation?" Bill asked as he stepped through the back kitchen door, Trenner Barnett close at his heels.

"Daddy!" Everett exclaimed as his attention was ripped from reminisces of Johnny Bradshaw's snot-rag to settle on the joy that his father had returned.

"Oh, Bill!" Lottie exclaimed, tears of relief spilling from her eyes to travel over her cheeks.

Savannah began to weep as well—weep with joy as Trenner's gaze fixed on her, as he strode to where she stood.

"Are you angry with me, Savannah?" he asked.

He looked tired, and his cheeks were red from

the wind and cold. Yet his dark brown eyes simmered as he stared at her with worry—with hope.

"No," Savannah answered, shaking her head. "I figured it out last night, while I was lyin' awake in bed worryin' over you. God did send you to us—to *me*—for me to love. And what better way is there to be led to the man you'll be in love with forever and ever, hmmm?"

Trenner exhaled a breath of being relieved yet said, "But I ain't a cowboy anymore."

"I know," Savannah said, stripping the tattered scarf from Trenner's neck and tossing it onto the table. "You're a deputy, a lawman. And I couldn't be more proud of you and what you have chosen to do as your occupation."

And it was true! Savannah had prayed long and hard at various intervals during the night—thanking God and His Son for sending Trenner and asking for comfort in knowing they would keep him safe in being a deputy. And the comfort she'd asked for had come: the moment Trenner had entered the kitchen behind her father, a voice had whispered to her mind that Trenner would always return from performing his duties as a lawman and, moreover, that Trenner truly did love her and was meant to love her—as she was meant to love him.

"Then . . . you still love me?" Trenner asked in a lowered voice.

Savannah brushed tears of joy, merriment, and peace from her cheeks.

"Of course I do! And more than ever perhaps!" she confessed.

Trenner's eyes narrowed, and in an even lower voice, he asked, "Will you marry me then? Will you marry me right now, right here, on Christmas Eve in front of God and everybody?"

"I will," Savannah answered without pause. She felt as if her heart had swelled to a hundred times its normal size as Trenner gathered her in his arms, kissing her cheek, her neck, her cheek once more, and then her lips.

"I prayed for comfort too," Everett said, tugging on Trenner's coattail.

Breaking from Savannah yet still taking one of her hands in his, Trenner hunkered down in order to be eye level with Everett. "You did?" he asked the boy.

Everett nodded. "I sure did. 'Cause you know I prayed for a cowboy for Savannah, so I was worried somethin' awful when you went and rode off as a deputy lawman last night."

"And what answer did you get from prayin'? If you don't mind tellin' me," Trenner prodded.

Everett smiled. "That once a man has been a cowboy, he's always a cowboy . . . at least in his heart. So it's all right that you're a deputy now, 'cause you'll still always be a cowboy deep down."

Trenner chuckled, stood erect, and tousled the straw on the top of Everett's head. "That's true," Trenner said. "That is indeed true."

"May I come in now, Mr. Barnett?"

Everyone looked to the kitchen door to see Reverend Allen standing on the threshold.

"Absolutely, Reverend!" Bill said.

As Reverend Allen stepped into the kitchen, closing the door behind him, he looked to Lottie, saying, "It seems we're to have a weddin' here in your home today, Mrs. Dickerson. What a great blessing indeed."

"A weddin'?" Lottie exclaimed.

She looked to Bill for direction, and he explained, "I'll tell you one thing—Trenner Barnett don't do anything halfway. When he sets his mind on somethin', he rides away like the wind. He asked me yesterday, before the social, if he could propose marriage to Savannah, and I said yes, thinkin' I'd have a bit more time to talk to you about it first. But then everythin' with the rustlers happened, and then Trenner was determined to marry Savannah so's they can spend Christmas Eve in the house in town he bought for them. And here I stand, without havin' had a chance to tell you all about it, Lottie. I'm sorry."

Lottie smiled, threw her arms around her husband's neck, and kissed him square on the mouth—in front of Reverend Allen and everyone.

"It's wonderful, Bill! It's just so wonderful! Thank you for knowin' my heart would've wanted you to do exactly what you did!" Lottie exclaimed.

"Are you ready then, Mr. Barnett? Miss Savannah?" Reverend Allen asked.

"Just a moment," Savannah said. Reaching out to remove Trenner's gloves, she stuffed them in his coat pockets. Then she removed his hat, tossing it to the hat rack nearby and ringing a hook perfectly with it. "Your coat, sir?" she asked Trenner.

Instantly, Trenner stripped off his coat, hanging it on the back of one of the kitchen chairs. He raked a hand back through his dark hair and smiled.

Savannah took Trenner's hands in hers and began walking backward, pulling him toward the parlor. "If everyone would please follow us into the parlor, I want to marry my man standin' in front of the Christmas tree."

"Because that's where Trenner first kissed you smack-dab on the mouth, right?" Everett asked.

"Yep," Savannah giggled.

Mere minutes later—there in the parlor in front of the family Christmas tree and with Savannah's beloved family to witness it—Reverend Allen pronounced Trenner and Savannah man and wife.

"You may kiss your bride, Mr. Barnett," Reverend Allen announced when the ceremony was complete.

"Thank you, Reverend," Trenner said, gathering Savannah into his arms. "I'll do just that."

"But kiss her good, Trenner!" Everett exclaimed. "Like you did that night out here in the parlor—you know, the night after the day Savannah fell in the bathtub with you? Kiss her that way!"

"Oh, I plan to, little brother," Trenner mumbled a moment before his mouth claimed Savannah's.

For an instant, Savannah was aware of her mother asking, "What is all this about Savannah bein' in the bathtub with Trenner, Everett?"

But that was all Savannah heard of the family's conversation—for she was wrapped in her lover's arms, in her husband's arms, and he masterfully crushed hot, impassioned kisses to her mouth, careless of who else was in the room.

CHAPTER EIGHT

Christmas morning dawned bright—clear, crisp, and with freshly fallen snow blanketing the earth.

"I can't believe you had all of this in place, Trenner!" Savannah sighed as she lay in her husband's arms. The fire in the hearth burned warm, crackling with comfort and adding to the bliss of the morning. "Even a Christmas tree? Our very own, our very first Christmas tree together," she said as she studied the beautiful evergreen standing in one corner of the room—entirely swathed in ribbon, berries, and especially mistletoe.

"I wanted our first night together to be special," Trenner mumbled.

Savannah rolled over in Trenner's arms. Smiling with joy and mingled awe, she placed her hand to his cheek, relishing the wonderful sense of his whiskers against her palm.

"But . . . you bought a house?" she giggled. "And a feather mattress? Put up a Christmas tree?" She paused a moment, placing a lingering kiss to Trenner's lips.

He smiled, gazing at her through narrowed eyes.

"Just being married to you on Christmas Eve . . . bein' married to you at all! There could be nothin' more special in all the world to me than that," Savannah assured him.

"Well, maybe the wife of a cowboy could expect to sleep on a bedroll out under the stars in the middle of winter," Trenner began. "But you're the wife of a deputy sheriff, so I figured the least I could provide was a roof over your head, a warm fire, a Christmas tree of your own, and a feather mattress to sleep on."

"So you plan to spoil me?" Savannah teased. Oh, his body was so warm, his skin so smooth, his muscles so chiseled and firm. She snuggled closer to him to relish it all.

"As much as I can," Trenner answered, "even though Everett was correct, you know."

"About what? God leading you to me?" Savannah asked.

Trenner kissed her lips sweetly—mumbled, "That too," against her mouth. Then he explained, "But I was thinkin' about what he said about me always bein' a cowboy at heart."

"That's right," Savannah giggled. Sitting up then and clasping the bedsheet to her chest to ensure her modesty, she reached over, retrieving Trenner's hat from her side of their bed where it had landed the night before when he'd undressed.

Plopping it onto her head, she said, "And Daddy said it too."

"Said what?" Trenner chuckled as he stretched out on his back, tucked his hands beneath his head, and studied Savannah.

"Daddy said, 'Well, I'll tell you one thing—' " Savannah had meant to complete her impersonation of her father with the words, *Once a cowboy, always a cowboy at heart.*

But she laughed when Trenner snatched his hat from her head, sat up, placed the hat on his own head, and, with his own impersonation of Bill Dickerson, finished the phrase with, "Rome wasn't built in a day . . . but I wasn't on that job!"

Savannah burst into giggles. "He does say that! Daddy says that all the time!" she laughed.

She continued to giggle, only this time with delight instead of amusement, as Trenner tossed his hat aside and pushed her back down to lay on the bed as he hovered over her.

"I love you so much, Savannah," he told her. "So much I can't hardly handle it. You know?"

"I do know," Savannah said.

Trenner kissed her, and it was his kiss of promise—promise that he loved her and that he was about to prove it to her once again.

"And I'll tell you one thing," Savannah sighed as Trenner's mouth moved to her neck—as he placed moist, lingering kisses to the hollow of her throat.

“What’s that?” Trenner asked in a whisper.

“I sure am thankful for the sweet soul and faith of a little boy I know,” she told him.

“Me too,” Trenner said, pausing in kissing her to gaze down into her face. “Oh, me too.”

AUTHOR'S NOTE

I've said it before, and I'll say it again: I totally believe in love at first sight! Or in the very least, I believe that two people *know* they're going to be in love at the moment they meet or when they reconnect as adults having known each other as children. I've seen it many times—with all three of my children, in fact—and I experienced it the moment I first laid eyes on my own husband, Kevin! Of course, doubt always, always plays a huge and very obviously negative part in each and every instance of "love at first sight." More often than not, the doubt comes not from the two people falling in love and knowing they want to or are meant to be together but from other people in their lives (i.e., family and good friends). It's a very difficult journey to make when you've known from the moment you've met your true love to the moment you can finally be married and together without everyone trying to belittle what you have or plant giant seeds of doubt that you know what you're feeling.

Yet the resulting relationships—drawn both from my own experience and in watching other people who have been blessed with the gift of "love at first sight"—are some of the strongest I have ever seen! In opposition of the doubt the world around you tries to flood your mind with, there is a deep psychological and spiritual connection that is so profound and rare that it motivates these couples to work harder on their relationship. It's like they have an extra assurance that they will be happy together, and because of that fact, there is actually less doubt about one another in their marital relationship than is more common in other marriages.

Oh, sure, this is just my own opinion. But aren't our opinions often formed out of years of experience, both personal and in observation of the experiences of others? Yes, they most certainly are!

Now, as far as the majority of the world goes, love at first sight doesn't mean a love is any less powerful, meaningful, or enduring. In fact, I think those who have the blessing of love at first sight overcome some challenges that those who don't are able to avoid. So whether you found your significant other with love at first sight included as part of your experience or not, simply be thankful for the fact that you did find it!

In this story, Everett is so much the child that many of us were—faithful, resilient, happy, and believing that anything is possible. Being battered around by the storm life tosses us into so many times causes us to lose that innocence, resilience, and faith. Of course, we have to lose it in order to deal with adult problems—in order to survive, really. But I think we can, and should, always endeavor to admire children for their profound wisdom and faith. They often offer great wisdom through simple words, right?

I remember one day almost twenty years ago I was teaching a group of kids at church; they were nine and ten years old. One boy was feeling particularly down one Sunday, and I asked him what was wrong. He explained to me and the class that he was tired of being "in the middle" in his family. His older brothers and sisters got to do all kinds of things he wasn't allowed to because of his age, and he felt his little brother got away with a lot because he was still the baby of the family.

As I began to formulate an answer that would soothe the boy, one of the girls in my class piped up with, "Well, you've got to realize that the baloney is the best part of a baloney sandwich . . . and it's in the middle of the sandwich! And an Oreo? Isn't the stuff in the middle the very best part of an Oreo? I think maybe you're the best part of your family because you're the middle . . . like the good stuff in the middle of an Oreo."

Wow, right?! I was astonished—awed! What

a wonderful little mind the girl had! What a positive spin on good old middle child syndrome! I've never forgotten that little girl's wisdom, if for no other reason than she found a way to be kind to that boy and make him feel special.

Anyway, I love that Everett's prayer was answered by way of Trenner literally blowing through the door to be loved by Savannah and love her in return. Things like that do happen! There *is* divine intervention in constant play all over the world! I've seen it in my own life, and I'm sure you have in yours. And after all, isn't that what Christmas is to us? The recognition and, yes, celebration of God's greatest gift to us, the greatest example of divine intervention—the birth of His Son and our Savior, Jesus Christ!

With that, I wish you a very merry Christmas and hope that this little Christmas novella made you smile, remember the faith you had as a child, and feel all those butterflies in your stomach that you had the very first time you knew you'd found your true love—whether at first sight or at the hundredth sight!

With Love and Best Wishes
for a
Happy New Year,
~Marcia Lynn McClure

Snippet #1—"I'll tell you one thing . . ." And there you have it: Bill Dickerson's familiar tagline. I'm sure you noticed its frequent usage through the book, and there is a reason for it. You see, when we lived in Monument, Colorado, one of the things introduced into our family vernacular was a comical little phrase that Kevin used whenever he was imitating a rugged old guy that worked for him named Bill. Bill was a military veteran, a wise and experienced man. He also spoke with thick Southern drawl, and many of his conversations with Kevin included Bill claiming he could do a job better, faster, and with greater skill than most people Kevin hired for similar work.

"I'll tell you one thing, Kevin. Rome wasn't built in a day," Bill would begin. "But I wasn't on that job!"

Therefore, after years of Kevin's impersonating Bill by quoting the man's *I'll tell you one thing . . .* phrase, our entire family adopted it. And yes, each member of our family, when using the phrase, always recites it with a heavy Southern accent—you know, for effect.

And there you have it—the real-life inspiration for Bill Dickerson and his tagline!

Snippet #2—Trenner's Name—Now, as you may or may not already know, my youngest son is named Trent. It's a rather long story—the story of how he came to be Trent. (I wanted to name him Maverick, but for some reason, Kevin wasn't on board with that. But when Kevin mentioned the name Trent—thinking of the 1992 men's gymnastic gold medalist Trent Dimas, whom I met when I worked for a dentist as a receptionist in 1985—and when Kevin reminded me that our son Mitch was named for the 1984 men's gymnastic medalist Mitch Gaylord, I agreed that I did like the name Trent. And so we named him Trent, middle name Adair, the surname of one of my Cherokee ancestors). Anyway, when I began writing *A Cowboy for Christmas*, the name Trenner popped into my head. Trenner is one of our son Trent's nicknames! He has many, of course, and they range from Twent, Twenter, Trenaton (as my father in-law calls him), Trentster, and even Pumpkin Seed (that would be the one I called him when he was little). Yet Trenner is one of my favorites of Trent's nicknames, and I thought it made a good cowboy and hero name. Don't you?

Snippet #3—Trenner's fever was worrisome indeed! Why? Because the two leading causes of death to cowboys in the Old West were riding accidents and pneumonia! Some historians even list pneumonia as the number one killer of cowboys. Sure, lightning strikes killed more cowboys than gunfights did, but I was astonished to find pneumonia listed as the most fatal element in cowboy deaths. And that's exactly why Lottie listened to Trenner's lungs and was so determined that he keep to the warmth of the ranch house until his fever passed—for Lottie knew the killer of cowboys that pneumonia could be! Smart woman, that Lottie.

Snippet #4—Johnny Bradshaw's Snot-Rag—Again, real life inspires fiction! When I was a child, my parents had some friends that would come to visit our family once or twice a year. David and Dana Porthouse (all names have been changed to protect the not-so-innocent) had quite a few kids, and one little girl was exactly my age. Her name was KristyAnne. Well, when I was about three or four and our family was living in Grace, Idaho, David and Dana and their kids traveled up to see us. Well, as young as I was, and as old as I am now, one of my most vivid memories of my young toddlerhood and of KristyAnne was her ratty old blanket/snot-rag. That thing was disgusting! And KristyAnne took it everywhere with her! I vividly remember KristyAnne and I laid out on the front room floor, having been tucked into having a little wee slumber party together during that visit. And I very vividly remember watching KristyAnne twist one corner of her security blanket/snot-rag, jamming it way up into her nose, and ringing it around in her nostril a bit before removing it to find the twisted corner not holding a gold nugget but a slimy wad of—yep, you guessed it—mucus! Bleck! To this very day, I still gag whenever I remember it! Eww!

ABOUT THE AUTHOR

Marcia Lynn McClure's intoxicating succession of novels, novellas, and e-books—including *A Crimson Frost*, *The Visions of Ransom Lake*, *The Bewitching of Amoretta Ipswich* and *Midnight Masquerade*—has established her as one of the most favored and engaging authors of true romance. Her unprecedented forte in weaving captivating stories of western, medieval, regency, and contemporary amour void of brusque intimacy has earned her the title "The Queen of Kissing."

Marcia, who was born in Albuquerque, New Mexico, has spent her life intrigued with people, history, love, and romance. A wife, mother, grandmother, family historian, poet, and author, Marcia Lynn McClure spins her tales of splendor for the sake of offering respite through the beauty, mirth, and delight of a worthwhile and wonderful story.

Books are produced in the United States using U.S.-based materials

Books are printed using a revolutionary new process called THINKtech™ that lowers energy usage by 70% and increases overall quality

Books are durable and flexible because of Smyth-sewing

Paper is sourced using environmentally responsible foresting methods and the paper is acid-free

Center Point Large Print
600 Brooks Road / PO Box 1
Thorndike, ME 04986-0001 USA

(207) 568-3717

US & Canada:
1 800 929-9108
www.centerpointlargeprint.com